SET ASIDE

A Second Chance Small Town Novel

KELLY COLLINS

Copyright © 2015 by Kelly Collins

No part of this publication may be reproduced, distributed, or transmitted in any form or by any means, including photocopying, recording, or other electronic or mechanical methods, without the prior written permission of the publisher, except as permitted by U.S. copyright law. For permission requests, contact kelly@authorkellycollins.com.

The story, all names, characters, and incidents portrayed in this production are fictitious. No identification with actual persons (living or deceased), places, buildings, and products is intended or should be inferred. All products or brand names are trademarks of their respective owners.

Dedication

For my Family

Chapter 1

HOLLY

Outside the prison, I sat and waited. Liberation felt overwhelmingly lonely. For the first time in decades, I'd face the world alone, and that frightened the hell out of me.

Thankfully, the universe was finally showing me a hint of a smile, and my heart thawed in the uncharacteristically warm October air. The sun was out, and the birds were singing, whistling freedom's ballad. It was funny how the birds sang outside the prison, but I'd never heard them on the other side of the fence.

Everything appeared softer, more inviting on this side of the yard. From where I sat, even the chain-link didn't seem as tall or foreboding. With my arms wrapped around my shins, and my chin on my knees, I watched the empty road ahead. Mickey was expected at eleven. I waited, inhaling the scent of car exhaust and grass clippings, the sweet scent of liberty. They were a welcome respite from the stale prison enclosure.

Around and around, I rolled my shoulders. A restless night in my bunk had left me with a stiff neck. My last night in prison, and it covered the spectrum of best and worst nights of my existence. Best because it was my last night, worst because I couldn't lie in my bunk anymore and dream about my future. I had to create one, and I had no idea where to begin. All I knew was, I must begin.

In the distance, a dust cloud rolled up the road. A hint of blue peeked through the nebulous dirt ball, a horn blared, and the smile I'd been missing since she was released from Cell Block C was there. With the finesse of a race car driver, the truck did a perfect donut and came to a stop in front of me.

"Hey, do you need a ride?"

"Let me think." I hopped from the cement steps, ready to go. "I could enjoy a lunch of mystery meat on hard bread, or I could have you take me for a burger." I gave her a *what-do-you-think?* look. "Gosh, Mickey, that is such a tough decision." I raced away from the prison toward the truck, toward the only friend I had outside the fence. "You were supposed to be here fifteen minutes ago." I teased, knowing full well she was early.

"You are so full of shit." She gave me a *get your ass in the truck* smirk while she eyed the small purse in my hand. "Do you need help with your luggage?"

I tossed the leather pouch at her head.

She ducked.

"Good dodge. I wouldn't want you to get a concussion from the sheer size and weight of my bag."

"Get in the truck, Holly; we've got shit to do."

It took about six seconds for Mickey to yank her buckle free and throw her arms around me once I entered the truck.

"Holy shit...are you really here?"

For the first time in months, I breathed freely. "Yep, I made it. Now comes the hard stuff." I held on to Mickey for way too long, but I felt if I let her go, she might disappear. I had missed her more than I thought possible.

Mickey pulled away and wiped at the tears pouring down her face.

"I'm so glad you're here. I have your cabin ready. Your letter said you weren't moving in with Matt. Tell me what happened. I wanted you to have your happily ever after. Lord knows we spent enough time in the bunks planning your life. We plotted it out so perfectly. You would live in your high rise apartment with your 2.5 children and ugly nanny. Holly, what happened?" Mickey's soft demeanor would change the minute I told her the truth about Matt. Mickey was a fierce and loyal friend.

"I'm not quite sure, but I have some suspicions, and I need to confirm them. Are you willing to help me catch the asshole red-handed?"

"I'm down for whatever you need. What are we up against?"

"I'm just looking for a few truths. Stuff doesn't make sense, and yet...it does. I'll know when I get there."

"I'm game. It's hard to believe you're the same girl they said wouldn't utter a profanity when she entered the system." Mickey snapped her buckle in place and grabbed the steering wheel. "Let's blow this hellhole."

I leaned over and turned the volume of the radio up, effectively ending our conversation about Matt. "I love this song." I swayed to the beat of the music.

"How is it you know modern music? I finished my sentence, which was half of yours, and I didn't know a damn thing playing on the radio." She grumbled something about music and fairness.

"It was a perk of working in the kitchen. We had a radio. Roz was partial to the oldies, but every Friday she played the top forty station as a reward for our hard work. It was our consolation prize for having to serve fish sticks."

She put the car into gear and eased down the road. "Where to, doll? I'm at your service." I turned around and watched my past fade from view.

"Take the freeway to Broadway, and then take exit 207A. The address is 2715 Broadway, Apt 2B."

"I could have called him to tell him we were coming. He could have had your stuff ready."

Duh. "If you're trying to catch a thief, you don't tell them you're coming. Same with a cheating, lying bastard."

"Oh my God, the asshole's been cheating on you? He doesn't know you're coming? Holy shit." Slack-jawed, she continued to drive. Her hands gripped the steering wheel, and her knuckles turned white.

"I didn't think he could keep it in his pants. I told him to break it off with me, but he said he would wait. Hell, I was so naive when I entered prison. I actually let him convince me." A laugh escaped, and I wondered if I'd lost my mind.

"Asshole." Mickey laid her hand on the horn and released a ribbon of colorful words at the driver who had cut her off. "Let me tell you, Holly, drivers haven't gotten better while you were in prison. I think the government released something in the air that sucked out people's brains."

Her mention of the brain had me thinking about the loss of my RN license. I reminded myself to grab my NCLEX study guide from the bookshelf when we got to Matt's.

"Lots of areas of the brain are engaged when driving, Mickey. The parietal lobe deals with spatial relations while the occipital and temporal lobes deal with both visual and auditory. Then there's the cerebellum . . ."

"You are way too fucking smart for your own fucking good." Mickey reached over and slapped at my arm.

"You're smart, too. You would sound smarter if every other word wasn't an expletive. What the heck, Mick? You're worse now than you were in prison. One thing I learned while there was that a carefully placed *fuck you* had a lot more power than a string of profanities." I shifted my head slowly back and forth. She really needed to clean up her act.

"Don't give me shit. I work with men on a ranch, and Kerrick likes my dirty mouth," her wet tongue slid out to ring her lips, "especially when it's wrapped around his—."

I slapped my hands over my ears and yelled, "Stop. I don't want to hear about Kerrick's penis."

"Oh, please, like I'd use that word. I was going to say co—"

"Christ. Cut me some slack. It's not like I've had the pleasure in two years."

"I'm sure you heard about lots of cocks in prison. I think Roz served it on Fridays, only she breaded them and passed them off as fish sticks. Right before I left, Officer Brady walked in the kitchen like the big dick he was and ran out like a pussy. What happened that day?"

I laughed at the memory.

"Officer Brady was tired of fish sticks. He came into the kitchen and told Roz to serve another meat. She told him that she had no other options. He grabbed his crotch and tugged, telling her he had some meat for her. She went for her cleaver, and he went for the door. Brady never came around the kitchen again."

"I wondered what went down that day. He always made an effort to steer clear of Roz. For an old buzzard, she managed to scare the hell out of the toughest guards. They gave her a wide berth."

Thoughts of Roz made me smile. "Did you know she was a prisoner for five years? When she finished her sentence, she applied for the kitchen manager's position. She's been there ever since—like twenty years. I couldn't imagine working there once I was released, but it showed me there was a future beyond the walls. She gave me hope."

Through the windshield, my old apartment building came into view. My heart pounded in my chest. Blood boomed like thunder in my ears. I wasn't sure I was ready for the confrontation, and yet it had to be done.

"Are you ready to do this thing?" Mickey threw the truck in park and stepped out. She'd never been this confident in jail. Freedom had done her good. Kerrick had done her good. I would never have pegged her as someone who would have hooked up with a cop. Life was exactly like fiction, strange.

Still used to being told when to walk, where to walk, hell, even how to walk, I moved slower. "It's now or never." Matt would sure be surprised that I showed up at our door a week earlier than expected.

When I met her out in front of the steps, Mickey cracked her knuckles like she was my strong-arm. "What do you think we're going to find?"

"If his schedule is the same, he'll be home. What I expect to find is someone else besides him." I pressed the button for 2B, took my keys out of my bag and snapped opened the lobby door. "Whatever slut he's been hooking up with." As the door closed, Matt's voice sounded over the intercom.

"Hello...hello...is anyone—"

The door clicked closed and silenced his voice.

Walking toward my former home, it felt as if the last two years had never happened. Same cracked floor tiles and broken mailboxes. Same slow ride up to the second floor. Same faded brown door that used to welcome me home. I closed my eyes. But two years had happened. Everything was different. I was different. I rapped on the door.

His footsteps thundered across the wooden floor. The door handle shook. A shadow crossed the peephole.

Nothing. Absolute silence.

I rapped again, only this time with more force. The deadbolt shifted. The door opened.

The color rushed from his face. "Holly." He stumbled back a step as if I were there to do him bodily harm, which wouldn't be out of bounds if busting his nose wouldn't send me back to prison. "Why didn't you tell me you were getting out early?" His gaze scanned the room like a guard looking for contraband.

"I wanted it to be a surprise." I skimmed my hand down his face as I walked past him and into my old home. It could be so easy to go back to status quo, but that was no longer an option. I wanted more from my life.

"It's definitely a surprise. A great surprise." He looked around the room and zoned in on Mickey.

"Matt, this is Mickey. She's one of my best friends from prison."

Mickey nodded and leaned against the wall. She didn't say a word. Her contribution to keeping him off kilter.

"Hi, Mickey." His greeting had the emotional equivalent of a piece of wood—hard and splintered. "Great to meet you." He wrapped his arms around my waist and put his sweet on. "Always loved these shorts. They're a cross between Daisy Dukes and cargo pants. My kind of perfect woman."

Set Aside

Before prison, his breath grazing my neck would have sent chills all the way down to my curlies, but now my butt clenched. With a clean twist, I outmaneuvered him and headed for the living room. The apartment was the same and not...it smelled different than the gardenia candles I'd burned. Now hairspray, lemon cleaner, and a cloyingly sweet perfume stank the room. I walked around, touching the things we used to share. Bookshelves full of medical journals filled one wall, but things were missing, too. Picture frames that used to hold our photos had disappeared. I thought I would feel sad walking into my *what could have been* life. I expected it to feel like a punch to the gut. All I felt was empty.

On the bottom shelf, my favorite nursing book was gone. Like I was never a part of this existence. Over the last two years, I'd been erased and replaced. Set aside.

"Where's my book?" My tone was direct and to the point. I was here for two things. The first was to get what belonged to me, and the second was to set free what was no longer mine.

"I put them away." He rocked on his feet. "I'll get them for you later." He paced the room. "How does it feel to be home?" His voice broke like a teenage boy.

This...home? I shook my head. Home was where the people who love you lived. Where you didn't have to be anyone but yourself. A place where you had value. How sad I had to be reminded of that in prison.

"It will feel better when I get these clothes off. Come on, Mickey, help me find something nice to wear."

Matt's face tumbled at the mention of clothes. I dragged Mickey down the hall to the bedroom that once had been Matt's and mine. Matt nipped at our heels. I knew my books weren't the only things that had been packed away, but watching Matt sweat gave me joy.

The lime green and orange pillows on the bed screamed shitty taste. Shitty taste wasn't Matt. He might be a selfish bastard, but good taste was something he always had.

"Holly, please..." He pushed himself in front of us, blocking the closet door.

"Save it, Matt. I know. I just needed confirmation."

His mouth dropped open, and I wondered if his reaction was because I knew, or because I hadn't killed him yet?

"It wasn't supposed to happen like this. Everything would have been back to normal by next week. It wasn't my intention to hurt you, to make you feel bad." His excuse was like Kool-Aid poured into a wine bottle. The color was pleasing, but the taste failed.

Mickey shoved him aside and yanked open the closet. "She doesn't feel bad; she feels free."

Matt gaped. "You gotta understand." His voice was whiney. "Everything would have been fine if you had stuck to the schedule." He deflated the minute Mickey stepped inside the closet.

Mickey rummaged through the hoochie mama dresses she would know weren't mine. She pulled a pair of jeans from the hanger and pressed them to my waist. Six inches too short. She spun on him. "Dr. Becker is it? I suggest you direct us toward her belongings. I spent a year in prison and almost killed my ex when I got out. I can't imagine what two years does to a girl."

"Right." He jumped like Mickey had lit his ass on fire. "I have your boxes down in the storage locker. Unfortunately, your Jeep isn't here. I can have it by tonight, if that's okay."

"You let someone borrow my Jeep? What the hell is wrong with you?" I could overlook someone in my bed. Letting someone borrow my car was another matter. "I want my Jeep back today, Matt. I also want my book. Who the hell needed my nursing book?" As soon as the words were out of my mouth, I knew who. Maybe not the exact person, but she'd be a nurse, and she'd be using my books and my Jeep, and that thought pissed me off.

"Holly, I'm sorry." His was a feeble apology. There was no muscle behind it; just the weak words of a liar.

"Mickey can tell you where I live. I haven't been there yet."

"We won't be home tonight," she damn near snarled. "We're celebrating, Rick's Roost for dinner and tequila shots. You'll have to make other arrangements." Her demeanor was sharp enough to cut paper.

"I know where Rick's Roost is; I'll meet you there, and we can all celebrate. The more, the merrier, right? Have you called any of your friends from the hospital? Carla is dying to see you."

"I just want my Jeep. As for Carla, I'll call her. Is she still in the same job—my job?"

His eyes looked around the room.

I glanced around, trying to see what he did. There was a romance novel on the nightstand, a bottle of perfume on the dresser, and a thong hanging from the drawer.

"Yes, she's the shift supervisor in the ER. She was next in line, and when you left, she was placed in the position right away." His face looked constipated, like he wanted to push out something too painful to pass. "How did you know?"

I walked over to the dresser and picked up the bottle of perfume. I spritzed a bit into the air and turned to walk away. "I smelled another woman's scent on you."

He ushered us out the door and into the elevator. "I got caught over a twenty dollar bottle of perfume." His shoulders shook as he laughed. Glad he could find humor in such a shitty situation.

"Bring my Jeep and my book to Rick's Roost tonight. Bring your girlfriend, I'd love to meet her. You can buy a round for everyone. We'll toast to new beginnings."

Mickey gave me a *you have to be kidding* look.

Matt had the smile of a kid who just got his way. I've always had a soft spot for his smile, and today was no different. He was a jerk, but he was a jerk with nice teeth.

Mickey shrugged her shoulders. "Why not? The bar is full of assholes. The more the merrier."

Matt helped us load several boxes into the bed of the truck. He pulled me into his arms and held me a little too long. I pushed away and hightailed it to my side of the truck. He followed.

"How do you want to split our stuff? I had an appraiser come in and give me an estimate when I updated the insurance. I'm happy to pay you for half. It would make my life so much easier. I'll even add an extra ten percent for the time it took you to pick out the stuff." He pleaded with me to say yes.

"That's fine Matt, whatever you think is fair." That response was an echo of the old Holly, the one who went with the flow and didn't ruffle feathers, but a clean break would be good, and I could use the money.

Mickey grumbled something like *Let's go* before she hopped in the truck and revved the engine.

"Ms. Impatient is ready. It's good to see you, Matt. I hope you're happy."

"Holly, you've changed. And those changes are attractive. Maybe we could revisit the thing we had. There is something incredibly sexy about your newfound confidence. You know, I think I could be happier." He moved in to kiss me, but I placed my hand on his chest, halting his progress.

"You're the past, and there's nowhere for you in my future."

Chapter 2

HOLLY

We drove under the M and M sign. Scrub brush and boulders dotted the landscape as we wound our way to the ranch. At the last turn, a large house greeted me with flower boxes filled with the final blooms of summer. On the far side of the field were several log cabins. Each one mirrored the next.

Mickey laid on the horn as we approached the row of cabins. She parked in front of cabin six. I had no idea why she was honking until a tall man with a perfectly trimmed beard strolled out of cabin eight. His brown hair caught the sun and showed hints of red throughout. His easy smile was that of a man who knew he was smokin' hot.

"What the hell is going on?" My eyes traveled to the man yelling from cabin seven. He could be a twin to the other man except for his clean-shaven face and deadly scowl. If he wasn't careful, the creases across his forehead could become permanent. Tall and intimidating, he made his way down the steps toward the truck.

"Holy mackerel, Mickey, who are you, and how did you get Chippendales to loan you men to work the ranch?"

"Nice eye candy, right? I think you'll like it here." Mickey jumped from the truck.

The two men exchanged words. The man from cabin seven looked annoyed, as if my appearance was inconvenient. The second man shook his head and walked to the truck.

"Let's get Holly settled in," Mickey shouted. "Carry her things into the cabin." She gave them a move-your-ass look, and both men stepped to it.

I'd never seen her command anyone to do anything, and I envied her take-charge attitude. I needed to harness some confidence to move my life forward.

The grumpy looking man snatched a box of my clothes from the truck bed and started toward the cabin. I swung the door open and exited, forcing the man to stop in front of me. His stare started at my legs and traveled past my stomach and landed on my breasts. I threw up my arms and wrapped them protectively around my girls.

I'd never felt more like porridge in my life. If Matt was Papa Bear, then this man was Baby Bear, and he hadn't been fed in days.

He dropped the box and scrambled to pick it back up. Several items spilled from the box, but it wasn't a big deal. I smiled, hoping to get a smile in return, but he tucked his head and walked away.

"Holly, the clumsy one is Keagan. He's Kerrick's younger brother. There are Keanan, Kerrick, Keagan, Keara and this here is"—she dropped her arm around the smiley looker—"is Killian. They obviously have a thing for K names."

Killian approached, offering his hand in greeting. "Ma'am."

I shook his hand. "Nice to meet you, Killian." And it was. I was relieved to know that I would have neighbors who were close by, even if only one of them was approachable.

Killian's eyes glistened under the high noon sun. They were an amazing blue-grey color, like a dove's wing.

Mickey grabbed a small box from the truck and guided me to the door. "Killian is usually the quiet one, but something has made Keagan mute." She looked over her shoulder and shook her head at the grumbling man.

"Are you twins?"

My eyes shifted between the two brothers, settling on Killian. At least he had looked at me. Keagan hadn't acknowledged me at all. I

Set Aside

would have loved to know if his eyes were the same color as his brother's, but more importantly, my ego could have used a boost. I would have settled for a sideways glance.

"No, he's older." Killian's answer was succinct, obviously a man of few words.

"These are the homely brothers. The good looking one belongs to me." Mickey led the way into my new home. "Put the boxes in the first bedroom." She nodded toward the hallway.

The men hustled to do her bidding.

Who was this woman who stood in front of me? What happened to the scared woman who left prison? I suppose she'd had the same baptism by fire I was experiencing now.

When Mickey said I could live with her, we were still in prison. She slept in the bunk across from me. With a bunch of vacant cabins at her ranch, she wanted her friends close by. The dream was we would all live on her property. I never imagined her vacant cabins would be modern houses. I pictured them as rough-hewn shacks dotting a desolate landscape. This was so much more than I'd expected.

I twirled in a circle, taking in the living room. A sofa, two chairs, a coffee table, and a television mounted to the wall. It was overwhelming. It was too much. It was perfect. I followed Mickey like a lost puppy to the kitchen.

She grabbed a couple sodas from the small but well-stocked refrigerator. The stainless steel appliances made my heart skip a beat. The coffee pot made it beat quickly. This was my kitchen. A place where I could enjoy a cup of coffee whenever I wanted. I debated powering it up so I could smell the freshly brewed coffee in the air, but she tugged me by the arm and guided me to the living room, where she plopped herself on the sofa.

"Have a seat. They can handle the rest."

The men made several trips from the truck to the house. Each time they passed, Keagan glared in my direction. I finally got a glimpse of his eyes. At first I thought they were blue, and then I saw the green. They were hazel, and they were simply beautiful.

"Anything else?" Killian asked in his rich, deep voice.

"Nope, thanks for your help." Mickey settled into the couch. "We're taking Holly to Rick's at six. Meet at the main house fifteen minutes prior."

The door snapped behind the men, and the silence descended. Mickey and I were alone.

For seven hundred twenty-four days, people surrounded me. The bells and alarms never relented. The lights never dimmed, the chaos never waned, and now there was only silence.

Mickey patted my knee in a motherly way. "Eerie, isn't it?"

We let the silence fill us until I couldn't take it anymore.

"What's with the tall and grumpy one? He seems to hate me already, and I don't even know him."

I took a sip of my diet soda. The carbonation felt good sliding down my throat. Diet cola was my guilty pleasure in prison. With everything changing, thankfully, some things remained the same.

"Don't know, but he'll snap out of it." Mickey shrugged with indifference. "The McKinley men literally saved my life when they set up business on the ranch of an ex-convict their brother barely knew." If a sigh could sound happy, Mickey just released one hell of a happy sigh. "Family loyalty is a priority for them. They have become my family. They will be yours, too."

Could it be possible to build a family again? I was envious of her ability to adapt to her life so quickly. "I want to be a part of a family again." My voice had a wistful edge to it.

"I'm your family, and this is your home. You are home, Holly." Mickey looked around the cabin, as if taking inventory. "You should have everything you need, but if you don't, let me know. I put a few surprises in your room. There are a variety of soaps and shower gels in the bathroom. I remember how good it felt to shower without rubber sandals. The grocery store is pretty close. I recommend going there as soon as possible. It was the one thing I did that made me feel normal again. That, and sex."

"I may be able to handle the grocery store, but having sex for sex's sake is a stretch for me."

Sex with Matt was good; not great, but decent. It was always about him and rarely about me. Sex was important, but it didn't top my list of things to do right away.

"I figured as much, which is why I left you a gift." She gave me a brow waggle and a laugh that was so free, I was envious all over again. Would I ever feel that free? "But seriously, I know you're hell-bent on getting your license back, but do yourself a favor and take a day or two to regroup and revive."

"You're right; I am tired." I laid my head against the sofa and closed my eyes for a moment. I really was beat.

The shift of her body caused me to open my eyes. She picked up the throw pillow and tucked it under my head. "It's funny how exhausting prison can be. We spend all day doing nothing but are always tired. I struggled when I got home and wouldn't have made it without Kerrick. The universe blessed me when it put me in his path." Mickey glowed every time she said his name.

I couldn't wait to meet this man. I hardly recognized the woman in front of me. She was still the sweet, considerate girl I had met in prison, but she commanded attention now. Strong, burly men answered to her, and she directed them like a drill sergeant directed his troops. She was in control. I wished I had a tenth of her confidence and an ounce of her courage.

"He sounds like a godsend." A pang of jealousy stabbed at my chest. She was so happy in her new family, and I felt more alone than ever.

"Well, I wasn't sure at first. At times he seemed like the Devil. He made me take stock of my life and forced me to look at the things I had. With his guidance, I was able to put my life into perspective. With his family, I was able to set things right. It's all new to me, and I'm making it up as I go."

"Thanks for taking me in, Mickey. I appreciate everything you're doing." She couldn't have known how wonderful it was to have a place to land. I had been uncertain of how my first day of freedom would go, but all in all, it seemed to have gone the best it could, given the circumstances.

Mickey lowered her voice as she lowered her head. "I haven't asked, but how are you dealing with the loss of your mom? She was your everything. I understand the loss, Holly. I'm here if you need me."

I lifted the pillow from beneath my head and dragged it to my chest. This would probably be the best hug I'd get in a while. "I'm adjusting. It'll take time."

"Okay." She slid off the couch and stood before me. "I've got shit to do. The ranch doesn't run itself; besides, you need to get settled." She leaned down and gave me a sisterly hug. I didn't realize how much I had missed her affection.

She left me alone to do whatever I wanted. There was no schedule, no routine, and no guards watching. I was free, really free, and I could eat at five in the morning or eleven in the afternoon. I could have a hamburger for breakfast or cereal for dinner. I was in charge of the remote control, the lights, and the temperature. My house. My rules.

After I investigated every room of my new home, I found myself sitting on the bed, looking at the boxes that contained my life. Twenty-seven years of living were shoved into nine plastic bins.

I fell back on the bed and ran my fingers over the beautiful Matelassé bedspread. Teal accent pillows cradled my head. I could curl myself up in a ball and bury myself for a week. I sat up, determined to unpack my life and begin again.

Mickey had thought of everything. She had gone out of her way to make the room special for me. She'd used my favorite colors and scents. She had welcomed me home.

On the nightstand was a three-wick gardenia candle. I raised the jar to my nose and inhaled. Memories of a different time floated through my head. My mother picking the white flowers from our garden. That was long before we moved to Colorado. I shook my head to erase the memory and placed the candle back on the nightstand. What a sweet surprise.

At the pace of a turtle, I unpacked the remnants of my past. Every dress I hung was a step toward my future and a notch in my confidence, confidence that took a hit when I opened the box of scrubs.

My heart tugged. I brushed my fingertips over the worn navy

Set Aside

blue fabric. Never a fan of the solid color, I couldn't argue with the fact that it hid blood and body fluids well.

I pulled a top from the box and brought it to my nose. I didn't know why, but I had always identified with smells first. They have a way of taking you places. Some people were visual, some people were hands on, and I was an olfactory girl.

My work clothes still smelled like softener. It made me wonder if Matt had washed my clothes recently. It was the kind of thing he would do. He was always good like that, doing nice things when I was ready to give him the boot. Maybe he washed them before he packed them away before he moved another woman into my home.

I sucked in a deep breath and let it out slowly. A lone tear slid down my face. I had worked so hard for a life with Matt, and the privilege to wear these uniforms, and it was all gone.

They said hindsight was twenty/twenty. When you love someone beyond yourself, it's easy to have your vision skewed. I hadn't seen clearly. I wasn't thinking straight. All I saw was Mom's pain, and I refused to let her suffer.

Knowing what I did now, I would have made different choices. We'd both lost everything that day. Too bad we hadn't been shown the consequences of our actions beforehand.

The open box of uniforms mocked me, reminded me of what I'd lost and what I had to recoup.

Over the next hour, I hung up my clothes and took side trips down memory lane. I visualized the places I'd worn my tight jeans and sparkly sweater. The Doctors' Ball where I'd worn my long gown. I fingered the cashmere sweater set Matt bought me for our first Christmas. We had been dating for about six months. He took me to this great fondue restaurant and asked me to move in with him. He seemed so sincere; I'd been so ready to take our relationship to the next level. Everyone loved Matt except Mom. She saw right through his sweet words and into his cheating heart.

The last box I opened was full of mementos. I pulled off the top and stared at the contents. The first picture was of my mom and me the day before I went to prison. Her eyes were bright and shiny, so was her bald head. I pulled the photo to my nose and inhaled. I wished I could smell her perfume. She wore something called *Fearless* from Victoria's Secret, and it was the perfect scent for her. I needed to buy some so I could smell her presence.

I would never forget that day. We spent it outside, eating BBQ and dancing to old fifties music I played from my smartphone. I knew she was exhausted. I also knew I would never have the opportunity to see her again, so I relished every moment. I was grateful to my lawyer for getting me released from holding to spend the day with her. I begged them to put me under house arrest until she passed. It was a first offense, but the judge wasn't feeling generous. Thankfully, I was allowed out on furlough to bury her.

I lugged the heavy box into the living room and positioned the photos on the mantel of the fireplace. The final photo of Mom and me got front and center. The rest got lined up haphazardly across the shelf.

With an hour left until I was supposed to meet everyone for dinner, I slipped into the bathroom to enjoy a nice, long shower. It was time to cleanse my body and soul.

Chapter 3

KEAGAN

I can't believe I'd let a woman get me so riled. She made my blood so damn hot, steam was frothing—and not just from my ears. From parts of me I didn't have the time to give attention to.

"Focus, Regroup. Re-engage."

I repeated the three words Dad had drilled into our heads whenever he caught us daydreaming. Daydreaming's for half-assers, and the McKinley boys aren't dreamers; they're doers. I pulled the catalog closer. This was the part of the business I hated. I wanted to be with the horses, working with my hands, but the equipment wouldn't order itself. Breeding would begin again in the early spring. As early as February, if I had my way.

I flipped the page with too much force and ripped the paper. Damn her and her tight ass and perky tits and a smile that could make a man forget his work. I pulled the torn page from the catalog and tossed it aside. There was nothing I needed on that page.

We preferred live cover for our breeding purposes, and who wouldn't? I shouldn't think of Brody and Diesel in the same way as I thought of men, but a live, soft vagina would always be preferred to a palm, or in their case an artificial vagina. There's nothing artificial about that woman next door. I mangle another page. AV is safer.

However, the AV is a must if we're going to maximize profit, and we need more than one.

The fifteen samples we shipped out over the summer netted the ranch over thirty grand. Add that to the eighty or so live covers, and we rocked out a solid income. Not too bad considering it was Killian's and my first year in service at M and M Ranch. We got started late and didn't have all the bells and whistles. This year would be different, but I had to stay focused.

On the order form I scribbled the number five next to twenty-two inch AV. Brody was well endowed and needed the extra room. I marked another five next to sixteen-inch AVs. Diesel didn't have as much pipe, but it worked just the same.

Thoughts of pipe made my dirty mind go directly to Holly. That woman was going to be a problem for me. She had everything I loved in a woman, from her blonde hair down to her long legs. *Damn it.* Thoughts of her were making my pipe twitch. I might have to borrow one of those new AVs if I was going to survive living next to her.

Focus.

I snapped the page forward. It tore from the force. This booklet would be in shreds before I was done going through it. Next in line were ultrasounds. Ultrasounds were a safe subject. They weren't sexual, and they were Holly free. At least I thought so until I began to wonder if Holly knew how to use one. Did she receive that type of training as a nurse? I pounded my fist on the table. The pages fluttered up, then settled.

Regroup.

Roland needed a good portable machine on-site. He was kind enough to bring his own over the summer, but if we wanted to offer premier services, we needed premiere equipment. I put a one next to the brand I was used to using. At three thousand dollars, it wasn't the cheapest, but it was easy to use and produced stellar images.

Semen extenders, funnels, shipping cartons. Her boxes, her smile, her long-ass legs. Ice packs. Yep, plenty of ice packs. I could go for a pack or two or ten. I ordered lubricant and about near burst out of my jeans. My attempt at distraction was a complete fail. Thoughts of Holly jumped from every page.

I flicked on the remote control to the TV and watched it come to life. Maybe mindless television was what I needed. The Hallmark channel would be perfect. I loved their movies because they were such bullshit. Who fell in love at first sight? I fell onto the couch and perched my feet on the coffee table. Lust...absolutely. Love...no fucking way.

I closed my eyes, took a deep breath and thought about horses and horseshit and damn ice packs riding my balls.

Somewhere deep inside, I wanted it to be that easy. Boy meets girl, boy falls for girl, and girl becomes boy's. The reality went something like this: boy met girl, girl blew off boy, boy chased girl, and girl fucked his best friend instead. Yep, lived that script already, but in spite of my experience, I still liked women.

I focused on the movie, hoping that the distraction would be effective. Of all places, the location for this film was a ranch, not unlike M and M. The girl was a photographer, and the man tamed wild mustangs. This was a movie for Killian; he was all about taming. I was all about breeding.

And the thoughts of Holly were back. In my screenplay, she was lying beneath me while I worshiped her body. Her long legs wrapped around my waist as I carried her into my room. At that point, the reel ran out. I couldn't let the rest of it play in my head. Another attempt at distraction failed.

I clicked off the TV and went to the kitchen to grab a beer, downed half in one gulp. Out the kitchen window, the setting sun blanketed the cabins in an orange glow. Next door, Killian screamed at the TV. I took another swig. From the sound of it, the Broncos' quarterback had thrown a pass that was intercepted, allowing the other team to score.

Holly's place was silent. It was like she had never arrived, hadn't invaded my peace with her long legs, her sweet voice, and thoughts of her vagina. She was probably napping. Or showering. Her thin body naked under a stream of hot water. I drained my beer and crushed the can on the counter. She would not be a distraction.

A shadow crossed her window, and I snapped up my chin. Holly stared straight at me. She was beautiful, a masterpiece in her own right. Silver strands ran through her golden waves, hanging past her shoulders. A perfect frame for her face. Fierce, and yet somehow soft blue eyes. Something about her icy blues warmed me. She mouthed *What?* and raised her hands.

My arms shook. My hands shook. My damn dick stood at attention. I stormed into my bathroom.

Fail.

Fail.

Failed.

Damn it. Life at the ranch had been good, predictable, orderly, and free of disruption. Holly showed up, and everything changed. I was no better than a teenager who couldn't keep himself under control.

I had pictured a tired, worn-out woman. Weren't ex-convicts supposed to look like they'd been ridden hard and put away wet? Sure, Mickey didn't look like that, but I assumed she was an anomaly. My preconceived notion was shot to shit the minute Holly got out of the truck.

I flipped on the cold water. I'm a grown man, for Christ's sake, and I should have more control. I had just enough time to hop into a cold shower and remind myself why I came to Colorado.

Focus.

Regroup.

Reengage.

As the icy water prickled my skin, I admonished myself. Gals like her didn't fall into my long-range plans. She was an ex-con with a felony conviction. I didn't care what her crime was. I didn't care whether it was justified or not. Her record meant very little to me, but it was the only thing I had left to dislike her for, so I would hang on to that like the horn of my saddle. I'd grip it with all the strength I had so I didn't fall for her. I had a lot of shit to do at the ranch.

Breeding.

Boarding.

Training.

Set Aside

My new mantra. Singularly focused on horses.

The ice water tamed the beast and sent shivers throughout me. Frozen to the core, there was no risk in having to show up at Mickey's with a raging hard-on.

The clock on the wall ticked, a second by second reminder it was almost time to go to Rick's. Dressed in jeans and a black T-shirt, I squirted on cologne and ran my hands through my hair. Ready, I stood against my entry wall and waited for her to appear.

She stared out the window only inches from my own, and her chest rose with each breath, as if she was sucking in courage. Her fingers slid through the strands of her hair.

Stunning, but tarnished. Focusing on her deficits was how I'd get through the night, the week, the month, the time it took for Holly McGrath to get out of my life.

With her back to me, she left her cabin and reached inside to turn the lock. I bet it was an interesting feeling to be on the other side of a locked door.

I waited a ten-count before I followed outside and suppressed a groan. She wore heels. Who the hell wore heels on a ranch? This wasn't Bloomingdale's. Ranches were potholes and cow shit and needed sturdy boots meant for hard work. This chick didn't belong here.

Another two steps, and she hit a pothole, her ankle folded, and I was across the space, catching her elbow before I thought better. Or she hit the ground.

Her heat burned into my flesh, and she stepped on another rock, tottering to the side.

I tightened my grip. "Be careful." My voice came out gruffer than I intended.

She shrunk into herself, hiding her blue eyes and losing her wicked smile. "Been a while since I wore heels." She forced a laugh that nowhere near sounded real. "I'll have it down in ten more steps." Her voice softened with every word until the last was a whisper.

I hated I noticed, and hated I had been so harsh. This woman twisted me like a pretzel.

"I'll get you safely to the house." I could practically hear the Hallmark movie "ma'am" on the edge of that sentence and feel her working to break my hold. I tightened my grip. "Don't make me disappoint my mother."

This time her laugh wasn't forced, and she stopped trying to get away.

Right before we got to the door, I stopped and stepped in front of her. She stumbled, nearly falling off her damn heels again. This time she grabbed my arm. Her touch was a welcome sensation to my body and a home invasion to my brain.

"We weren't properly introduced." I kept my tone distant and polite. I needed to get this, whatever it was, on professional terms. "I'm Keagan McKinley. I'm the official breeder here at the ranch."

Her eyes snapped up to meet mine. "Stud Services?" Another giggle slipped. "How does one interview for a job like that?" She stepped around me and knocked on the door.

I liked to flame with the shame of a school kid with a crush on his teacher. Had I really just told her I was the ranch's official breeder?

Mickey and Kerrick stood in the doorway. Mickey bubbled while she introduced Kerrick to the beautiful blonde. It was like kindergarten, and today was show and tell. Killian snuck up on Holly, slid his hands around her waist, and planted a smooth kiss on her cheek. He looked at me with a cocky grin my knuckles were itching to make disappear.

That's the problem with brothers. They know everything. It's not often I got flustered, but this woman had me completely turned inside out, and there was no way Killian didn't notice. He was going to milk that for everything he could. My next plan of attack would be escape and evade.

Kerrick and Mickey filed out of the house and headed for his truck. *Great*, now I'd be stuck in the back seat with Killian and Holly. How was I supposed to ignore her if she was sitting next to me, smelling like coconut pie?

She followed Killian, and I followed her. She was right, it took her about ten steps to master those heels. I stared at her legs while she walked to the truck. The sway of her hips kept me mesmerized until Kerrick tapped me on the shoulder and pointed to the other side of the truck.

A groan escaped; how embarrassing to be caught staring by my big brother. I hung my head and rounded the truck. We slid inside from opposite ends. Out of the corner of my eye, I watched her dress slide up her thigh.

My fingers tingled at the thought of running them from her ankle to her hip. Her skin looked as smooth as a new foal's coat...*damn it.*

I shifted in my seat. My zipper pressed uncomfortably into my swiftly growing erection. As soon as we got to the restaurant, I was going to hit the bar. *I needed a drink—a few drinks if I were to get through this night.*

Chapter 4

HOLLY

Keagan jumped from the truck the minute we arrived at the bar. He acted like he wanted to get as far away from me as possible.

I leaned toward Killian. My feet were already hurting in my heels. What had made me think they were a good idea? What had I done to piss Keagan off? "I don't think he likes me very much." I picked at the hem of my dress. What did I do to Keagan besides show up?

"Don't worry about my brother." Killian offered me his arm. "He doesn't know a good thing when it bites him on the ass."

Like I was a real lady and not some ex-con straight from the Denver Women's Correctional Facility, he escorted me into Rick's Roost and stopped inside the door. He scanned the darkness, then gave me a slight bow, a hand squeeze, and an "I'll be right back." With swift assurance, he headed straight to Keagan and slugged him in the arm. I pressed back against the wall. I would never understand the relationship between siblings. As an only child, I had no idea how the dynamics of family and birth order worked.

The music from the jukebox played loudly. The smell of hot wings filled the air. My stomach growled. It had been so long since

Set Aside

I'd been in a restaurant, longer since I'd spent time out with friends.

Neon signs hung above the bar. The colors were vibrant and happy looking. So many things to see. The people, the pool tables, the dart boards; it was all a bit overwhelming.

Kerrick peeled off from our group and walked to the bar, where Killian and Keagan stood. I followed Mickey to an empty booth in the corner.

"Did the girls beg you to drink tequila shots for them?" Mickey looped her arm around mine. "Do you remember I had to drink a shot for each of you?" She rolled her eyes. "I don't recommend four followed by several more for good measure." She swayed like she was drunk.

"Nah, I got drunk on the chocolate liqueur bottles Natalie snuck in. I'll start with a diet soda. Matt's bringing my Jeep." Her lips puckered in an unflattering way. I knew she was unhappy about him coming, but he had something I needed.

"Keagan," Mickey called to where the brother's lined up oldest to youngest, as if they were required to stand in birth order. "Can you drive Holly's Jeep home? We're getting our drink on."

Keagan's expression was stone-like. When Killian leaned into his brother, he got a punch in the chest. And Mickey got a hard nod.

"No, Mickey," I said. The man had already made it clear he didn't like me, and now he was forced to babysit me. "He should be able to drink if he wants."

"He'll be fine. Tonight is about you, not him. Let's have fun. You've been contained for a long time. Don't you think it's time to let loose?"

I'd never been a let-loose kind of girl. The one time I acted impulsively got me incarcerated. Nope, I'd hang back and watch.

Keagan walked back to the table with a scowl on his face and an empty hand. Killian and Kerrick followed behind with a pitcher of beer, glasses and a soda for Keagan.

Hazel eyes inspected the bubbly brown drink. "Fine." He slid into the booth opposite me and shot me a black look. "I'm the designated driver."

I turned away, feeling uncomfortable under his glare.

"Here's to friendship and family." Mickey raised her glass. "I love you all."

We tapped glasses together and mumbled our here-here. With the beer at my lips, I looked over the rim directly into Keagan's eyes. His movements mirrored my own. We challenged each other silently. He was surly and unfriendly, but there was something soft and alluring to him. He was a teddy bear you wanted to hug, then punch.

Was it his aloof demeanor? Lots of men were standoffish. I was never attracted to that type of challenge.

Was it his sky-meets-sea eyes? Lots of men had hazel eyes, but his were a mixture of two vibrant hues. They were mesmerizing to look at. The kind of eyes that held your attention the minute they focused on you.

Maybe it was the smell of his cologne. Outdoorsy pine mixed with his own musk was the perfect blend for him. It matched him. I wasn't sure what to expect, knowing these men spent their days with big beasts and lots of horse poop. I certainly didn't expect him to smell so nice.

"Holly, this is Roland." Mickey waved her hand in front of my face as if this wasn't the first time she'd said my name. "Holly?"

I dragged my gaze from Keagan.

"Roland's our vet, and he helps with the horse breeding on the ranch." She looked proud when she talked about the goings-on at the ranch. "He's in charge of sending specimens to ranchers who want to artificially inseminate their mares."

"It's nice to meet you." I shook Roland's hand. It was amazing how Mickey had turned the ranch around in a few short months, but then again, she had a village of warriors at her side. And despite their epic good looks, Keagan was definitely the most impressive. I gave my attention to Roland. "I'm one of Mickey's projects."

"So you're Mickey's new project?"

He smiled in a way that didn't condemn, and I liked him. Blond curls and eyes the color of buttered rum and warmth exuded from every pore. He was surely worth more of my time than...Keagan.

"Yep. She is determined to help me get on my feet."

He shoved into the booth next to me. Keagan grumbled something about boundaries.

"Mickey and I go way back to when we were kids. She's a good one. And I'm sure you're not just a project. Mickey is never done with the people she loves and respects. You've gotta be a keeper."

I wasn't sure if it was the mention of family or the half a beer I drank while I wasn't paying attention, but a tear slipped down my face. I tried to swipe it away before anyone noticed, but Keagan narrowed his eyes as if he were trying to figure something out.

"What did you do time for?" Keagan's question jumped in, and my heart took off like one of Mickey's well-bred horses.

I wrapped my hands around the cold mug and stared into the amber liquid. So good to be free. So good to be surrounded by people who were nice. I glanced at Keagan. At least some were nice, and now the not nicest wanted my story. I could skate or come clean. I squared my shoulders. "I was arrested for purchasing drugs with the intention to distribute." I wasn't proud to admit it, but I owned it.

"At least you're honest." His shoulders rolled forward, and his eyes dropped down to stare at the table. I felt his disappointment all the way to my insides.

"My mama always said the only time to be less than honest is when someone's feelings are at stake."

"I disagree." His smug expression tucked behind his glass of soda. "Honesty is imperative at all times, regardless of feelings."

"Really?" I leaned forward into his space. "So let's lay it on the table. Why are you being an asshole?" His chin jerked up, and his eyes flamed. "I haven't done a damn thing to you, and you've done nothing but treat me like I walked out of prison, carrying the plague."

There was nothing like silencing a table. Mickey, Kerrick, and Roland tilted their heads in unison. Keagan placed his soda back on the table, and Killian sat back with an I've-got-a-secret smile.

I ignored him and his secret. As much as I disliked Keagan's smugness, at least he was honest. I wish I had the courage to swipe the smirk off Killian's face. He may be ruggedly handsome, but there was something too knowing and too in control about his demeanor for my tastes.

"Prison is your plague." Keagan jerked to his feet. "I don't want anything to do with it. I'm outta here."

Every mouth at the table fell open. Mine damn near hit the floor. So, he hated that I was an ex-con. I could understand his distaste. It left a bitter taste in my mouth as well.

"At least we all know where we stand." I grabbed the pitcher and filled my mug. If I had to endure censure and hate, I'd rather do it drunk.

"Don't pay attention to him." Kerrick touched the back of my hand. "Something has him all excited and agitated." He chuckled, sipped his beer, and shared a glance with Killian, as if enjoying their secret, and I wondered if it was at my expense or Keagan's?

"Two years for a first offense." Killian ran his thumb around the rim of his mug as if he expected there was far more to my story than I'd given. "Normally, you'd get probation."

I'd hoped for probation, community service, and a huge ass fine, but the judge wasn't in an accommodating mood. "I was caught buying the drugs in a school parking lot."

The "ahh" that escaped his lips said it all.

"How did you get that contact?" Kerrick, in full detective mode, began the interrogation. "I don't know anyone who would be stupid enough to sell drugs in a school zone. It's an automatic two years."

"You don't have to tell me the minimum sentence. I served it." I still remember the police cars surrounding me. I had the Ziploc bag of joints in one hand and a wad of twenties in the other. "My mom was terminal and in pain. They told me pot could help." It was an excuse, but I'd broken the law. "I had no intention of selling the drugs."

"I'm sorry to hear about your mom."

Kerrick's condolences hit my heart with the force of a runaway boulder. Mickey was a lucky woman. I avoided a rush of tears by changing my focus.

Across the room, Keagan stared at me from the pool tables.

Set Aside

He shrugged and mouthed the words *I'm sorry*. His face looked sincere, but I didn't know if my heart could trust him. He pointed to the open table and raised his brow, throwing me an olive branch.

I gulped my beer. A dangerous branch. A branch that could break my barely mended heart. I took another gulp and stood.

I shouldn't fold so easily, but I wanted to know more about this man. He ran cold, but now he was offering warm. I wanted to see what warm felt like.

I squeezed myself out of the booth. "I'm playing pool." Mickey waved me off and told me to have fun.

Just short of my destination, I rolled my ankle and found myself falling forward into his arms. One day free, and I was determined to break my neck. Embarrassed, I looked behind me to see if anyone noticed my less than graceful exit. Everyone at the table appeared to be occupied by conversation.

Keagan steadied me and looked down at my feet, "You're going to kill yourself in those heels." Lowering to one knee, he slid my shoes off.

Left barefoot, I chose a cue and leaned against the table. "I thought you hated me?"

"I don't know you." He grabbed the triangular frame and racked the balls. "Eight ball, wanna break?"

Disappointment washed over me. I didn't know what I'd hoped for. "I'm not a good player."

"Then I'd best break." He gave me a sly look, like breaking the rack wasn't the only thing he was interested in torturing, and I couldn't help wondering what it would feel like to be trapped in this man's hands.

I shook off that thought before he saw where my mind had gone. "Be my guest."

He placed the white ball at the end of the table. With precision, he sent it in the perfect position to displace the racked balls. Several balls fell into the pockets. This game would go quickly, and I would lose without an ounce of dignity left.

He made his rounds on the table, turning it over to me when he missed the fifth shot. I lined up the cue ball to hit the number eleven. I'd hoped it would head for the right-hand pocket.

"Are you trying to lose?" He chalked up the end of his cue. "If you wanted out of the game, all you had to do was say so." The way he eyed me felt as if he were asking me about more than pool.

"Told you. Not good at games." And I couldn't even begin to understand the rules of the hot/cold game he had going on. "Give me facts. Give me a pathogen, and I can tell you how it enters the body or how it mutates. How a disease takes hold." I knew about cancer, pain, and the loss of someone I loved. I knew about doing whatever it took to ease someone else's hurt. "But ask me to give you a precise angle or backhanded game, and I'm lost." I bent over the table to take the shot that was guaranteed to go in the opposite direction I'd intended.

"Wait." He came up behind me and leaned over my body. He placed his hands over mine. The heat of his body flooded through me. It was hard to focus with him so near. "If you hit the ball right here, it will shoot to the right. You don't want to hit it too far on the left, because it will go directly right, and that's too severe an angle to make the shot." He pointed to a place on the ball. "Find the sweet spot, and you'll be fine."

Fine. Fine. Fine was a feeling I'd all but given up on, and finding his sweet spot...well, that wouldn't come close to being fine or easy. I swallowed the tightness in my throat and steadied my shaking hands. Lining up the cue, I smacked the white exactly where he said. The white smacked the blue striped ball and glided into the corner pocket.

"Amazing." I jumped up and down like a kid who'd won the spelling bee. "I'm a pro." I danced around the table. Maybe fine wouldn't be so hard after all. "What should I sink next?"

"Don't get cocky. To win, you have to be committed." Committed was something I couldn't do. Not to him. Not even to Mickey. I had other commitments that needed my attention. Getting back my license. My test. My flipping life.

"Go for the orange striped ball on the left." He pointed to the orange thirteen sitting at the opposite end of the table. "Shall we up the ante? Put something on the line?" He pulled his lower lip into his mouth.

I almost dropped my stick. I'd be damned if that wasn't the sexiest thing I'd seen in a long time. "I've got nine boxes to my name. What do you want?"

His eyes lit up. "Information. Let's play." He grabbed his cue. His long legs filled out the black jeans perfectly. Too bad his disposition wasn't all that pleasant, because everything else about him was nice—really nice.

"Information?" I asked. "You realize, I'd tell you anything if you only asked."

He paced the length of the table.

"So...are you game?"

With nowhere to go and nothing better to do, I said, "Yes." Maybe I could learn something about him as well.

I hit the ball exactly in the place I thought I should. If I had eyed it right, it would bounce off the white and into the pocket. Unfortunately, the ball went too far left and missed the mark.

"How tall are you, Holly?" He grinned like a boy who'd just touched my boob.

"I'm five feet, eight-and-a-half inches." What a silly question. Of all the questions he could have asked, he wanted to know my height? "Do you want to know my weight, too?"

"Would you tell?" The slow sweep of his eyes from the tip of my toes to the top of my head had me squirming. If I didn't know better, I would have to say this man found me attractive.

"Um, I think I'm around one hundred forty pounds, but it's been a while since I've been weighed."

He sliced the cue ball, sending the solid red into the far pocket.

"Mom says a man should never ask a woman her age or weight."

"Your mother is a smart woman. I'm twenty-seven, by the way." Old enough to know better than to get involved with this man, but young enough to risk my heart again.

He lined up the cue ball and took his shot. The orange number five slid into the center pocket. Damn it, he had earned another answer.

"Are you a drug addict?"

The cue stick shook in my grip, and my palms went sweaty. I'd never considered anyone would think that of me. Anyone who knew me never would have asked that.

"No." I leaned the stick against the wall and gripped the table to stop my shakes. "I've seen what drugs do working in the emergency room."

"Why the buy?"

"If you hadn't stormed off in a huff, you'd already know." I eyed the table, wondering what ball would be his next victim. What question would he throw? "Besides, I imagine Mickey already told you my story."

He lined up the cue and sank number four into the lower corner pocket. "Mickey believes everyone should tell their own story."

"My mother got cancer, and I couldn't watch her suffer anymore."

Silence. Silence dripping with disappointment. Disappointment I couldn't take anymore. I'd broken the law. I'd helped my mother. I'd done my time. Who was he to judge? I had to get the hell away from Mr. Hot/Cold and fast. I ditched the game and darted away before he could drop another probing question.

I turned to my right and ran straight into a wall of muscle.

I looked up and said, "Matt," my I'm-so-glad-to-see-you smile slipped, "and Carla." The beer in my stomach sloshed uncomfortably. I totally didn't expect that. Carla my friend, was the one who took my man, my bed, and my job?

Chapter 5

KEAGAN

Holly staggered backward like she'd been kicked by a horse. The blood drained from her face, leaving her skin the color of death. Her toes pointed toward the door, and I wasn't sure if she would stay or bolt.

"Matt, you're here. Did you bring my Jeep?" She looked past Matt to the woman standing behind him. She winced like she was in pain.

Matt's arms circled Holly's waist and slid down to pat her ass.

Fury drove me to her side, but she pushed Matt away before I needed to intervene. I stood straight and broadened my chest. Let the asshole try that again, and he'd get a piece of me.

"Hey, I used to love it when you were barefoot and nearly naked." Matt's laughter filled the space. "Did you dress down for me?"

I'd give him a dressing down. One that included my fist in his face if he didn't back the fuck off. The girl behind him seemed to feel the same. Daggers shot from her eyes, but I wasn't really sure if they were directed at Holly or the asshole. These two needed some serious lessons in manners, but going all whoop ass on either of them probably wouldn't be the smartest move.

I dropped my arm around Holly's shoulder. "Nope. She dressed for me." I pulled her to my side. "She's mine." Holly stiffened under my arm.

"Holly...yours? Wow, two years in the pen has lowered her standards. You're just a cowboy." His tone was condescending. He intended to get a reaction. He got one, not the one I was dying to give him, but a toned-down version because there were ladies present.

I shot him a look that said *back off* as I pushed my chest into his. I'd been taking crap from my brothers all day long, and I wasn't about to take shit from this asshole.

Holly stepped between us. Was she protecting him or me? "Actually, Keagan is the official breeder for M and M Ranch." She spoke with pride, and it made me stand taller.

I tossed my head toward the chick behind him. "Who's your girl?" The poor thing was left standing in that asshole's wake without so much as an introduction or acknowledgment.

"Holly's friend, Carla." Matt introduced her like an afterthought. Just Carla. No claim. Her shoulders slumped, and she shook her head. A sigh slipped past her lips. She appeared hurt by his lack of enthusiasm.

"Holly, take your friend and get a beer." It hadn't been my intention to sound so gruff, and I didn't like the way her cheeks heated. She appeared to weigh my demand before she acted. She watched me over her shoulder as she walked away.

I wanted to punch that son of a bitch so badly, my knuckles itched. I didn't like the way he looked at Holly. I didn't like the way he ignored his girl. And I didn't like the familiarity of his touch. It was like he knew exactly where to place his hands for the best fit on her body, and that didn't sit well with me.

I tossed the pool cue on the table. I didn't like that I didn't like any of that. "Dammit." I'd publicly claimed her, and I didn't want her thinking I was interested in a relationship. I wasn't. Not with her. Not with anyone. I didn't have time.

"Hey man, you up for a game?" I asked the jackass in front of me. He was dressed like a Gap mannequin. His white pants were rolled up, showing off his boat shoes and bare ankles. His pink button-down cotton shirt was rolled up at the sleeves. What happened to good old jeans and T-shirts? Real man clothes.

"Sure. I'm Matt, by the way. I'm Holly's fiancé." He didn't offer his hand to shake. He turned his back and pulled a cue from the wall.

"You mean ex-fiancé. I'm pretty sure I saw you walk in with another woman on your arm."

"You mean Carla? She was a good distraction while Holly was in jail, but I'll have Holly back in my bed in no time." He chalked his cue and waited. "I haven't tapped that enough. She may be pissed at me now, but she always gets over it." His cocksure smile grated on my nerves.

"You're a dick." I racked up the balls and handed him the cue ball. What I really wanted to do was shove it down his throat. I didn't know Holly well, but even an ex-convict deserved more than this guy.

"All guys are dicks. If you're not a dick, then you're a pussy. Which are you?" He took the cue ball and sent it careening into the rest. In spite of the good break, nothing dropped.

"You want to play for something?" I egged him on.

"Are you talking money?"

"Information."

He appeared to be sizing up my intent. I had no intention of going after Holly, but he didn't know that. I wanted to know how far he'd go to screw up a life or two.

"You don't stand a chance, buddy. I'm a doctor. You're a…" He gave me a look that said he had no clue what I was. "Battle's won." He analyzed the table, looking for his next move.

He was out of moves. "Humor me."

"All right, I'm in."

I broke the rack and chose stripes for Holly, since she had them last and my first sunk in the corner pocket. "What kind of medicine do you practice?" If I kept him talking, he wouldn't focus on the table. That would give me an edge.

"I just finished a fellowship in gynecology."

"Well, then being around me should be a breeze. You're used to dealing with pussies."

I second-guessed my decision not to shove the ball down his throat. I took the second shot, landing the nine in the corner pocket, then gloated.

He leaned against the wall, crossed his arms and legs. "Your ball, your question."

"Why travel a path you've already walked?"

"You don't know, Holly." Matt flagged down the cocktail waitress and ordered a drink. His hand slid over the curve of her ass as she walked away. His leer, the perfect look for a lecher. "She's forgiving." His tone was matter-of-fact. He played on the weaknesses of others to press his agenda.

I clenched my cue so hard, I felt the wood give under my grip. A hair away from beating the shit out of this guy, by the end of the evening he'd wish he had studied proctology.

"She's a gorgeous woman; she could do better than you." Hell, she could have dated a toad, and it would have been a step up. This man was not Prince Charming; he was Prince Harming, and it was easy to see how he'd leave a path of destruction.

"I doubt that. She has little experience with men, less experience with standing up for herself. Did you know she doesn't even cuss?"

The waitress brought his drink. He handed her a twenty, telling her to keep the change.

"Naw, man, we're just getting to know each other." Obviously, our little Holly had changed in prison. I'd heard several foul words slip past her luscious lips tonight. Lined up, I was ready for my next shot.

My chalked tip touched the ball. "Too bad you won't get any of that," he blurted. My cue slipped off the side of the white, and it rolled without direction until it stopped in front of the fifteen. "Don't know what two years in prison will do to a girl, but I bet she's as tight as a virgin. I'm looking forward to popping her reborn cherry."

"Your turn." My voice was clipped and direct. I just wanted to get this over with. Get Holly back to her cabin. I wanted to return to my status quo.

"What does a cowboy make these days? I can't imagine it's much." He lined up his shot and waited for my answer. He was just another educated imbecile. People mistake hard work and horseshit with destitution and dumb. Most ranchers I know pull in a respectable income. I was college educated, not some grass chewing stereotypical mockup of a cowboy.

"This has been an off year with my midyear move to Colorado. I imagine I won't pull in more than sixty grand when it's all said and done." I waited until he'd pulled back his cue before adding. "But I made three hundred fifty grand last year."

He fell into the table, sending his ball rolling slowly to the right. "No way. You made three hundred fifty grand fucking horses?"

"No, if I were fucking them, I would have charged more. I have a degree in animal husbandry from Texas A&M. I make my money by breeding winners. Do you like horse racing?" I leaned against the table. "What about the rodeo?"

He cleared his throat like he was choking on something. My success. He didn't appear as confident or cocky. Maybe medical school siphoned common sense out of his brain and left stupid in its place.

"I love the track. How do you make that much money breeding horses?" He braced the table and leaned toward me like I had some secret. The secret was hard work and focus, something I was finding hard to do with Holly around. I glanced in her direction and caught her staring at me. Her lips were pulled taught. She appeared to be having as much fun as I was. Not.

I looked back at Matt and almost felt sorry for the idiot. He probably sat in an office filled with posters and models of reproductive organs. He'd be several hundred-thousand-dollars in debt and got there because of his love for vaginas. Maybe he had just crossed the six-figure income index. His lost look told me he couldn't understand how a cowboy could be worth more than him. I was more than a fucking cowboy. I could see his synapses firing, telling him he was a loser.

"Two years ago, a horse named Lucky Duck won the Derby. I bred her when I was twenty. She was trained to race. At three years old, she took it all. I've been breeding world-class racers for years. Now I'm moving on to rodeo stock. People pay a lot for my sperm." *Chew on that, you cocky bastard.*

"That's amazing. So what brought you to Colorado?" He began to pace the length of the table.

My inner cowboy kicked up his spurs and relished in Matt's discomfort. My outer one stayed quiet and calm, waiting for his chance to lead this idiot to slaughter.

"Family. My brother needed me. I came."

"You're confident you can repeat the magic here with rodeo stock?" He sipped his beer and waited and waited and waited.

It was fun to watch his assuredness waiver and fall. "It doesn't take confidence; it takes skill. I know horses, and I have an amazing family. That's a winning combination." I ran the rest of the table, leaving Matt in the dust. With my cue put away, I left him standing alone.

I walked slowly to the corner booth. Everyone at the table appeared to be enjoying light conversation except Holly and Carla. They sat like two opposing chess pieces stuck in a stalemate.

Killian rose and pushed me into his place next to Holly. "Hey, something came up. I gotta run. She's had a few beers, make sure she gets home safely."

"Yep, I got her. Who came up?" It had to be a woman. It was always a woman with Killian.

"Trish...she's been very naughty."

I would never understand his predilection for girls who needed direction, but I was happy to have him leave. Holly didn't need the attention of man-whores or lechers. Getting rid of Killian took care of the first. I'd have to figure out something for Matt.

The seating arrangement had changed while I was away. There was Holly, Carla, Roland, Mickey, and then Kerrick. Mickey, Kerrick, and Roland were in deep conversation about the barn conversion. Holly and Carla sat in silence. As soon as Matt approached, he pulled up a stool and took a seat. Carla perked up.

Set Aside

When his eyes focused solely on Holly, Carla deflated.

"Have you talked to the board about your license?" Matt asked Holly.

She tore a cocktail napkin to shreds and added it to the mountain already in front of her. "I have an interview tomorrow."

"You know I'm here to help in any way I can." His lips rose into what I assumed ladies would call a swoon-worthy smile. My eyes drifted to Carla, who was scowling, and not completely directed at Matt.

"I'll probably need a few character letters. I was hoping you could write me one." Holly's voice sounded hopeful.

I grabbed an empty glass from the table and poured myself a tall one. One beer couldn't hurt, and I desperately wanted this one. I understood the need for professional references, but there had to be someone else who could lend her a hand. Surely, she had more resources than these two.

"I'll write one." He looked at Carla. "You'll write your friend a letter to help her get her license back, won't you?" It was less of a question, and more of a demand.

Carla's gaze bounced between Matt and Holly. "Sure. What's your ultimate goal?" I'd never trust a tone as sweet as saccharine.

Holly remained silent for a minute. "I want my license back. I want my job back. I want a normal life."

"I have your job." Carla's voice filled with concern. "Surely, you don't mean to displace a friend."

It struck me as funny to watch this woman fear being displaced when she had so easily replaced Holly in every facet of her life.

"Your position isn't the only supervisory job in the hospital." Holly was cool and aloof. "I'll find something else." She flicked the napkin confetti, sending it across the table.

Mickey, Roland, and Kerrick stopped their conversation. The shredded napkins fluttered around them.

"So, let me get this straight." I found my voice after being left nearly speechless. "You ended up in prison, lost your nursing license, lost your job, and lost your fiancé? Now your 'friend' has your job and your fiancé. Next thing you know, you'll find out it was some sinister plot to take over your life." I couldn't help myself. The laugh erupted on its own. This shit only happened on television.

Carla's face fell. She burned like an ember getting ready to spark.

"You're not funny, and that's not nice." Holly pushed me with her shoulder.

"I'm not being funny, she fucked your man while you were in prison. I bet she lived in your house and drove your car, too." By the looks I received, I knew I had hit a bull's-eye.

Carla began to cry. Her eyes pleaded with Matt. "Are you going to let him talk to me that way?"

"Well, babe, it's kind of the truth. Holly was only in jail for a week before you started panting after me." Matt leaned back and balanced the stool on two legs.

My leg jerked like it wanted to kick that damn stool out from under him, but I ground my heel into the floor. This wasn't my fight.

"Fuck you, Matt, and Holly, fuck you, too. I don't need this shit. I don't regret anything." She poked Holly in the arm. "You always had it easy. You got everything. I got nothing. Finally, I have something, even if he's an asshole." Carla inched toward Holly and me, making us slide out of the booth. "Holly, your NCLEX book is on the passenger seat." She turned her head toward Matt, who was still perched precariously on two wooden legs. She pushed on his shoulder and sent him rocking to the ground.

Perfect.

Everyone turned, watching Carla storm off. I watched Holly. It was obvious she was hurt by the betrayal of her friend and ex-boyfriend, but there was something in her expression I recognized. It was the look of determination, and I was confident she would be okay.

"Matt, you hardly seem like the frustrated ex who broke up with your girl. You sit here and stare at Holly like she's a T-bone and treat your girlfriend like she's canned meat."

Matt slid back onto the stool, not saying a word. I liked him better on the floor.

Holly shifted so close, our legs touched. That little spark of defiance I saw a few minutes ago was slowly fizzling.

Call me an ass, but I continued. This time, I questioned Holly. "Most women would have clawed the eyes out of the woman who stole her man while she was in prison. Can you help me understand why you sat here and said nothing?"

Matt's shoulders shook from his laughter. "Is that what she told you? She's was always looking out for others. She was probably trying to protect my ego." He reached over to touch Holly, but she snapped her hand back as if she'd been touched by fire. "Holly tried to let me loose toward the end of her sentence. I thought I'd convinced her otherwise. I'm trying to convince her it was a mistake."

Her head flew up, and her shoulders pulled back. She looked like a bird ready to peck his eyes out. "Don't talk around me like I don't exist. You were fucking someone. I had no idea who at the time. Now I know, and it's unforgivable." She leaned over the table and got into his face. "I don't know if I'm more angry at you or her." She let out a growl that would make a pit bull proud. "Just give me the check for my stuff and leave. If you hurry, you might catch your ride home." Holly pushed off the table and collapsed back into the booth.

"Oh shit," Matt said. He pulled a folded check from his back pocket and tossed it on the table before he ran for the door.

Holly grabbed her purse and scanned the group. "It was nice meeting you, Roland…Kerrick." She focused on Mickey "We'll talk later."

Mickey reached for Holly's hand and gave it a squeeze. "Yes, we will."

"Let's go, Keagan. I've had enough."

Chapter 6

HOLLY

I yanked open the passenger door and stopped. Sitting on the black leather seat was my book. The Nurse Practitioner's Study Guide taunted me with all I wanted. All I might never get back.

I snatched the book from the seat and held the tattered cover close to my chest. My nails clawed into it. I knew this stuff. I knew how to be a nurse. That's who I was. The feel of the weight, the smell of the pages, was enough to take my anger down a notch.

Down, until I climbed in. My once pristine car had seen better days. Empty soda cans and candy wrappers littered the floor. My Jeep smelled like Carla. I yanked the heart hanging from the rearview mirror. I couldn't look at a symbol of love when I was full of rage.

"I'm sorry." Keagan reached over and ran his fingers down my arm until his warm palm covered my cold hand. "You deserve better."

"I had no idea." The damn cover ripped in my grip. "Carla had always liked Matt, but she never put a move on him when we were together."

That wasn't exactly true; she was always on the verge of being a bit too friendly, but I overlooked her longing looks and seemingly innocent touches because she was my friend. Friends were supposed to have your back, not put a knife through it.

"Bullshit. She moved in on him the day you left. There was no loyalty."

I twisted in my seat. "Well, you know that rumor about hindsight." I didn't understand why he cared. It was my life, my past. "It's time to move on."

Keagan's laughter filled the air. "You're a piece of work. Letting him off the hook so easily." He adjusted the seat to accommodate his long legs. "You needed him, and he failed." He let go of my hand, put the Jeep in gear, and backed out of Rick's. "Expect shit, and you'll get shit."

If I were a violent person, I would have backhanded him. "I'm drowning here, and all you want to do is hold my head under the water." I tossed the damn heart in the backseat. "I'm aware of my mistakes. I can't solve everything on the first day."

"I'm not trying to drown you." Keagan spun the car out of the parking lot. The sky was darker than my mood. "I'm just telling you what I see. Those two are nothing but trouble, and we don't need more trouble at the ranch. Mickey has dealt with enough. Anything that hurts you will hurt Mickey."

My insides tore, not because his warnings had nothing to do with my feelings, but because he thought I was a threat. "I love Mickey." My voice took on a you-gotta-believe-me tone. "I'd never do anything to hurt her or compromise what she's worked hard to achieve."

"This situation is a mess." He pressed his fisted hand against the steering wheel and cracked several knuckles. "What you do and who you associate with affects everyone."

"Are you finished?" I slammed my hand on the dash. This situation appeared darker than the starless night.

"No, I'm not finished." He sat stone-like with his eyes on the road. "Your mama sure set you up for disaster, pretending the world was rosy. Open your eyes, Princess. The world is waiting."

"Don't talk about my mother. You didn't know her, and you have no right to judge." I wanted to bury myself. I wanted to cry. I could have opened the door and jumped. The pain from the asphalt would have hurt less than his words. The memory of my mother was sacred ground.

"I'm not trying to be disrespectful. I'm sure your mother was wonderful."

"I've seen the world, and I know it's not pretty, but my mom taught me to love unconditionally, to look for rainbows." Out the front window, the headlights ate into the darkness. "Might serve you to learn a bit more about compassion and understanding." Keagan had spoken earlier of loyalty. No one knew loyalty more intimately than I did. This man should be so lucky to have my loyalty.

He parked the Jeep in front of my cabin, shoved open his door, and tossed the keys into my lap.

"Now I'm finished." He slammed the door, and the silence covered me like murky water. I wasn't sure if I wanted to fight anymore, but I wouldn't give Keagan the satisfaction of witnessing my failure.

Woozy with drink or emotion, I eased out of the Jeep and wobbled to my porch. I didn't even glance back at him. I didn't need his help, his advice, or his protection.

He'd said he would see me safely home, and he had. His responsibility ended.

And that was just fine by me. I slammed my door, thunked my book on the table, and slouched into the couch. The cushions swallowed me, and I liked the way they held me, hugged me.

There was nothing but stillness and an occasional hum from the refrigerator. No bunkmates snoring. No cell doors slamming. No guards yelling. I missed the commotion. A house without people was so empty, and I had never been a solo act. I snuggled deeper. Another thing I'd have to get used to. Spending time alone. Spending time by myself.

You could be sharing a bed with someone and still be alone. There was a time I thought Matt and I were happy. Who wouldn't have wanted the love of a man like him? He was smart, handsome, and successful. He worked in my field. He understood me. He wanted me. I'd wanted to be wanted.

Which wasn't the same as a real connection. I'd always been present, but he'd been absent. I'd been *give*. He'd been *take*. My poetry to his prose—lots of prose.

Had he ever looked at me like Kerrick looked at Mickey? I couldn't say for certain, but I think I would have felt it if he had. I hated to think Keagan could be right. Did I pretend the world was rosy because everything I had was the best I could get? Did I settle? Something resonated deep inside of me. They say the truth hurts, but I never expected it to have cut so deep or felt so bad.

I threw a pillow across the room, knocking a newly placed picture on the mantel. To hell with Carla, and Matt could screw himself. The NCLEX book was a bully who refused to be ignored. When I opened the book, it was bound to be painful. I would be eviscerated if denied my license. Four years of schooling would have been wasted. I'd never considered anything else. Telling me I couldn't nurse was like telling a dog it couldn't bark.

I grabbed the book and flipped through the pages. Several were earmarked. Page twenty-seven had a note from my mom that said, *you've got this*. Page one hundred had a smiley face with its tongue stuck out. Page one hundred seventy-six had a heart with the words *your mom loves you* scrawled through the center. I flipped the book to the back, and my mom had left a note five years ago, the day before my original exam.

My darling Holly,

It doesn't matter what happens. What matters is how you handle it. There is no doubt in my mind you will pass your boards, but if you don't, it's not the end of the world. Sometimes, we make plans and the world has other ideas. You are an amazing woman, an amazing daughter, and an amazing friend. I've been so lucky to love you. Close this book, honey, and live your life. This is not the last chapter, it's the beginning of the sequel.

With all my love,
Mom

One tear followed another, and another, and another. "I love you, Mom." Mom would always be there for me.

I tossed the book aside and focused on the pictures that lined the fireplace mantel. My story started with sadness, moved through joy, and settled itself in sorrow. I dragged myself from the couch and walked to the pictures. The scarred wooden shelf held the milestones of my life. Twenty moments of happiness framed for posterity. No one could take those memories away. They were etched into my soul.

Echoes of Keagan's voice floated through my head, *Open your eyes, Princess. The world is waiting for you.*

He was right. I'd let myself down. Settled for so little when I deserved so much more. I would never allow that to happen again. Tonight, I would cry myself to sleep. Tomorrow, I would move forward with my life.

I rubbed my swollen eyes. Too tired to do anything but go to bed, I sank into the mattress and purged my miserable soul.

Chapter 7

KEAGAN

Killian didn't come home last night, so the morning chores were all mine. I was in for a rigorous workout. Twenty stalls of mucking shit and rotating horses between the pasture and the arena.

Over time, I'd pinpointed different personalities, and I knew which horses could be trusted to play nice. Some were shy, some were bullies, and some were sweethearts. Too bad people weren't so easy to read.

I led the golden-haired mare into the pasture. Her mane, the color of Holly's hair, blew in the breeze. If Holly were a horse, she'd be one of the sweet ones. The mare bolted when I set her free, and I imagined Holly felt happy to be free. I'd been wrong about her. She wasn't stupid. She was too nice. She was too damn frustrating. I patted the mare's hindquarter and let her run. Holly couldn't see I'd only been trying to nudge her in the right direction so she could be free.

Sweaty and hot, I pitched horseshit into the corner and mentally imprinted Matt's face on each pile of dung. I laid down new bedding and moved into the next stall.

By noon, my head was coming off my shoulders. With Holly wailing half the night, I hadn't gotten any sleep.

Scoop.

Throw.

Scoop.

Throw.

The pile of shit was getting higher and deeper.

Her crying had twisted my gut. It took everything I had not to rush in and pull her into my arms last night. Instead, I closed my window so I wouldn't interrupt her private moment and headed to bed. I left her alone. This morning, I felt like I'd abandoned her.

I threw another shovelful onto the dick-face pile. Abandoned her just like him. She had no one but Mickey, and I hadn't helped the situation by attacking her from every angle. She needed more. She needed a friend, a loyal friend. And around here all she'd gotten was me. I shoveled another load of crap. I wasn't going to be just another asshole. I wanted to be something better. More.

I approached my cabin with a new mission in mind. She wasn't going away, so I'd need to figure out how to make it work.

She backed out the door, dressed for the boardroom. However, if she were stripped of her pants and jacket, all that would be left was a white shirt, her undergarments, and those black heels. Yep, she would be ready for the bedroom. *Damn it, not going there. I'm going to be a friend.*

"Good morning." I watched her come off the ground by inches.

She swung around and looked at me. "You scared me. Make some noise next time." She locked the door behind her.

"Sorry, that wasn't my intent." I couldn't help chuckling. Scared probably wouldn't come close to how she'd feel if she knew I had a key to all the cabins.

"Just a bit touchy, I guess."

"You look nice." Nice was a stretch; the puffiness from crying couldn't be camouflaged, but she was still damn beautiful.

"Thanks." She looked down at the porch and rocked back and forth between her feet.

I dug my hands in my pockets and tapped my boots against the step. Did talking to me make her nervous, or was it something else that made her uneasy?

"Where are you off to all dressed up?"

"I have my first meeting with the licensing board." She bit her upper lip and chewed the edge.

I dug my hand deeper in my pocket. I swore I could see her mouth turn red and swell. I licked my lips and thought about the other ways to make her lips red and swollen. I leaned over to wipe the dust from the toes of my boots. At least I wasn't staring at her lips anymore.

"Do you want to eat here tonight? I'm barbecuing some burgers, and it'd be nice not to eat alone." One minute I was dusting my boots, the next my mouth was running like a wild mustang.

She looked at me, the Jeep, back at me, and then the porch.

Was I so awful to her, she couldn't stomach having dinner with me? I was trying to make up for my initial shortcomings.

"Why?" She cocked her head to the side and looked at me like a confused puppy.

"I'm not a bad guy, and I want to prove it." I swiped at the moisture running down my forehead. I'd worked all morning and hadn't broken a sweat, but standing in front of Holly, I turned into a leaky faucet.

The stiffness in her shoulders relaxed. The crease that had formed on her brow flattened. "Sure, how about I bring dessert?" She didn't sound fully committed to the exercise. It was more of an *I don't want to be rude* yes than an *I'd love to join you* yes.

"I like chocolate. Do you want beer or wine?" Her face turned white, and I laughed.

"No alcohol for me." She groaned as she rubbed her hands across her stomach. "I'm not usually a drinker, and I think my liver is pickled from last night."

"You had three beers." Lord, if she thought three beers could pickle her liver, then I was well on my way to being completely preserved.

"Yes, and that's three beers more than I've had in years."

"I suppose we'll have to work on that for future nights at Rick's."

"Only if you'll teach me to shoot pool." Her voice dropped low, like pool was the last thing on her mind, and I'd be damned if my dick didn't begin to twitch. Why was it the minute I saw her, my pants began to choke me like a serial killer?

"Yeah, sure." I stepped to the side, trying to adjust myself.

"Sounds like fun. Maybe I could win a few questions. There's a lot I'd like to know." She looked at her watch, "I gotta go, but I'll see you tonight." I watched the sway of her hips as she walked to her car.

"You can ask them tonight," I called after her. "I won't even play you for them." She peeked over her shoulder. I'd hoped she would smile at me before she left, but she simply looked in my direction and drove away.

And my dick took a nosedive. Yesterday, I'd had a carefully laid out, no serious relationships, no distractions, just work plan. Holly had thrown everything off-kilter.

She'd been here a day, and the minute she left I'd felt her absence. Life on a ranch could be lonely.

The clanging of the chain always gave him away. I barely got in my door when I heard Killian walk up my porch steps. He wore the stupid chain around his belt buckle. It looked like a dog collar. I had never asked him what it was for, but I had a pretty good idea it played in with his kink.

Without turning around, I yelled, "Come in." He was halfway through the door before I got both words out. "What do you want? Are you out of bread?" I dragged a loaf from the cupboard and took the bologna from the fridge. Killian generally shopped at my house.

"Nope, but if you're offering lunch, I won't turn you down." He plopped down onto the chair. "I just came over to see how things went with Holly last night?"

My chair scraped across the linoleum when I pulled it out. The legs creaked under my weight.

Tight-knit families were tough. If I raised an eyebrow, someone would notice, and they'd know the exact thing that had caused it.

"It was fine." The stupid little bastard wanted to get up in my shit.

Out of all the men in my family, I was probably the one most likely to stay single. Keanan would certainly marry if he met the right girl. Kerrick married once, and I definitely saw him heading in that direction again with Mickey. Killian would eventually settle down once he found someone he could conquer.

I pulled two slices of bread from the bag, avoiding the crusty ends, and shoved the sandwich fixin's toward my brother. He could get his own plate. I wasn't his wife.

"You like her. She's got you all riled up. You're coiled tighter now than you were when you fell for pucker-up-Patty as a kid."

"Shut up. Patty was a whore. Holly's not. Holly's nice enough, but nothing special." Which was a lie, but Killian didn't need to know Holly had smarts and a heart to go along with her hot body. Damn, I was still trying to forget her leaning across the pool table.

"She has a great set of tits and a glorious ass. If you don't move on that shit, I'll be forced to go in for the killin'." His smug smile was like a target on his face. Why couldn't my parents have named him something like Ken? Going in for the ken had less impact.

I fisted up and aimed for his smart mouth. "You're an asshole, Killian." He pulled a Matrix, and I barely grazed his chin.

"That fact has never been contested." He shoved the rest of his sandwich into his mouth.

He rocked his chair onto two legs, and I kicked his seat, ass-planting him good. "Big ones fall hard." Catching Killian off guard had never been easy, and his retribution was hell. "No time to play." I was at the door before he was off the floor. "We have to set up the foaling stables." I headed for the barn in a hurry.

Outside the barn, Roland was ready for work. He had become like a brother to us. If he wasn't blond, we might have been able to pass him off as a McKinley.

"Hey man, how's it going?" Roland looked ready to work in his tattered jeans and boots. With four mares birthing at the end of summer, converting the barn had to be a priority.

To my left, Killian raced straight toward me. It was seconds until impact.

Oomph. The air left my lungs as he flattened me with a body slam. Once he got his punch in, he dusted off his jeans and bro-hugged Roland like nothing had happened.

"Something I should know before we pull out the power tools?" Roland lifted his brow and offered me a hand.

"Naw, we don't always agree. We're brothers," I said.

Killian took another swipe at me, but I saw it coming and deflected.

"He says he's passing on Holly. I say he's full of shit." Killian stepped out of hitting range.

"I'd move on that. She's hot." Roland cupped fake breasts, the universal sign for a nice rack. I better not find him looking at Holly's rack, or I'd rearrange his pretty boy face.

"You, too?" I shook my head in disgust. "You're killing me."

"Don't bust his chops, or you might find a fist in yours," Killian said as he rubbed his chin.

"Shut up. She's fine. We're having dinner tonight, and that's all I'm saying. Let it go." I turned toward the barn door so I didn't have to see their faces. Their hoots and hollers were enough to make me want to kill them both.

Chapter 8

HOLLY

The aisles were filled with chocolate options. Cake, cookies, ice cream, and candy filled the shelves. And I was supposed to choose? They even had chocolate-covered potato chips. I pulled a box from the shelf and read the ingredients.

"Yuck."

Chocolate milk, cocoa puffs, donuts, and fruits. If that wasn't enough to stump a girl, I now had to choose a type of chocolate. I felt sick inside. There was milk, dark, and white, which wasn't chocolate at all. Add in flavors like orange, cayenne pepper, and mint.

I clutched the empty shopping cart. Research was needed. "Excuse me," I said to a Keagan-aged cowboy, strutting the aisle.

"What can I do for you, ma'am?" He pulled his hat from his head, and his smile was warm, might have been sexy, but evidently grumpy men were currently my thing.

"What chocolate would you recommend for our first date?" The words were out, and my cheeks flamed.

"Sweetheart, you can bring anything, and I'll be happy." Hungry eyes devoured me like I'd been dipped in chocolate.

"We don't have a date. I have a date with someone else." I pushed my cart to the side, ready to move on.

"I'm heartbroken; we've just met, and you've dumped me already."

"You're not being helpful."

"I'm offering you what I have."

"I don't want what you have, I want a cake."

"Well, there you have it. You've made your choice, and as much as it pains me, you didn't need me."

"Thanks for your help. Any favorites?"

"If you're goin' for cake, I'd do the chocolate sin. Sin is the only way to go." He reached over and picked up the cake dripping in dark icing and placed it in my cart. It did look decadent. To his credit, he seemed to know his chocolate.

"If your date doesn't work out, I can pick you up tomorrow for dinner. What's your number, doll?" The man was as smooth as a rocky outcropping.

I might have fallen for his corny line and boyish good looks. Flattery could get you just about anywhere, especially with a girl who's been locked up for years.

"I really need to get back to the ranch." There should be a litmus test for men so women can bypass all the bullshit.

His expression sagged, and he clutched his chest. "I get it. Always a few seconds late out of the chute." He backed away and tilted his head. "What ranch are you headin' to?"

He was just a guy, being a guy, and yeah, I'd been flattered. He'd been flirty and nice. Two things I wasn't used to anymore.

"I just moved into M and M Ranch." Without a thought, I gave him more information than he deserved.

"I'm sure I'll see you around again. By the way, I'm Cole."

"Nice to meet you, Cole. I'm Holly. See you around."

With the cake in my basket, I walked every aisle of the store. I didn't need much. Milk, juice, and corn flakes, Skittles and Pixie Stix, reminders of happier times. But even with a near-empty cart, it felt good to be free.

It helped clear my mind of the morning meeting.

Set Aside

In spite of the tension churning inside of me, the meeting with the board had gone well. The damn letters of recommendation requirement were going to be a stumbling block, but it wasn't a surprise. I'd figure it out. Maybe I could backpedal and get Matt and Carla to help me out. It wasn't the best scenario. Needing them for anything was difficult to stomach.

One night at a time. That was my chant. The days were easy; the nights nearly impossible. As soon as the darkness covered me, loneliness invaded. I was not a woman who could live in isolation.

"I'm going to have to deal." I spoke loud enough for several customers to look at me. Yes, I was talking to myself. Embarrassed, I fled down the aisle and turned into the produce section.

Fresh flowers filled one corner, and I inhaled. Roses and lilies scented the air. My eyes were fixated on purple irises and baby's breath. Color had a way of making my spirit soar. I plucked my favorites and moved forward.

Bright orange pumpkins sat near the door, and a silly thought crossed my mind. With six of them loaded in my cart, I was looking forward to Halloween and the pumpkin carving contest we could have at the ranch.

After a stop at the phone store, I'd be free to go home. *Home...*it had only been two days, but I was already settling in. It was amazing how a night full of tears could turn into a day full of happiness.

Which lasted me all the way back to the ranch, across the pebbles, and to my cabin's front door. I scanned the area. Trucks crowded in front of the barn, but there wasn't a cowboy in sight. Of course, I wasn't looking for just any cowboy. Not finding Keagan, I didn't let disappointment creep into my heart. I'd see him tonight.

I unlocked the door to *my* house and spun around to take it all in. *Mine.* I could hardly believe my luck. I'd never been able to call anything mine. Foster care, then Mom, then Matt. Never on my own.

Who would have thought I would get such joy out of a menial chore such as unpacking groceries? But I was full of bliss as I slid the milk onto the shelf and arranged my flowers in a jar I'd found under the sink. Hell, doing laundry excited me. Simple chores—simple pleasures.

Chores complete, it was time to explore my surroundings. Maybe Mickey could spare a few minutes and have a cup of coffee with me. She needed some straightening out about my breakup with Matt.

When I left the house, I didn't bother to lock the door. I felt safe. Comfortable. The pumpkins sat like chubby orange soldiers on my porch. The swing swayed in the breeze. The air seemed fresher. My step felt lighter. The sun seemed brighter. I was filled with hope.

Voices coming from the barn attracted my attention. Keagan's voice boomed above the rest. I was drawn to him like a magnet to metal. I approached the barn and listened.

"The new guy gets here tomorrow. He can start framing out the birthing stalls after he cleans the boarding ones. Killian and I will be able to help in-between our normal chores."

"We're getting another boarder, so we've moved Diesel and Brody to the staff stables behind the cabins. The new guy has two horses he'll house back there, too," Killian said.

"The dude's a roper. Wouldn't it be great if we could start some clinics here soon? It could be fun inviting the 4-H kids in for a junior rodeo. A lot of them will never make it to a real one, so if we could grant them a wish, I think that would be cool." Keagan's voice softened when he was discussing horses and children.

I peeked my head into the barn. "Hello."

Keagan gave both men the look my mom referred to as stink-eye. Not a look I wanted to see on any face, but when he turned toward me, he had a smile.

"How did it go?" His calloused hands ran down my arms. My skin prickled beneath his touch. Goosebumps the size of bubble wrap rose on my arms.

"It was good, all very positive."

He pulled his hand away and adjusted his Stetson. He looked damn sexy. In fact, Keagan had a raw masculine quality that would rival any man in a suit any day.

"You still up for dinner?"

Set Aside

My full attention focused on his tongue, darting out, licking at his lower lip. I had a vision of those lips covered with chocolate, with me doing the licking.

He waved his hand in front of my face, cutting off my vision. "Holly, are we having dinner?"

I shook my head. "Yes, I'll be there. What time are we eating?"

"How about five? I'll start the grill, and we'll visit while I cook."

"Sounds perfect."

The barn seemed awfully quiet. Killian and Roland were leaning against the wall, staring at us. As soon as they saw me looking, they turned and started talking about horses.

"Ignore those idiots." He wrapped his hand around my arm. "I'll walk you out." The heat of his palm sent a sizzle through my body. "So what are you up to now?"

"Heading to the main house to see if Mickey wants some company. Maybe she'll make me a cup of coffee."

We walked together across the field. Each time I brushed against him, I felt a jolt of awareness. He caught me by surprise when he gave me a chaste peck on the cheek as we reached the door. The only problem was, my body reacted like he had laid me down and ravaged me. My heartbeat rushed, and my skin flushed.

"I'll see you tonight." He rocked back and forth between his boots and shoved his hands in his front pockets. Gone was the tough cowboy, and in his place was boyfriend material.

"I'll see you tonight," I mimicked.

Perfectly filling his jeans, he walked back to the barn.

When I turned around, Mickey leaned against the doorjamb. Her expressive eyes asked a million questions. I was in for the interrogation of a lifetime.

"Shall we stand here and stare, or do you want to come in and explain why my future brother-in-law looked like a teenager stealing his first kiss?"

Caught in the act, I had nowhere to go but inside to confess.

"We definitely need to talk. You make the coffee, and I'll spill." I came for advice, but I'd tell her anything she wanted to know.

Mickey pointed to the table and headed to the kitchen.

Dutifully, I sat. Her house was warm and welcoming, and I loved the place immediately. A path from the front door to the kitchen was worn into the hardwood floors. Family photos decorated the walls. It had a homey feel. Anyone would be comfortable coming in, kicking off their shoes, and staying for a while.

She placed my cup on the table and sat across from me like old times. When she'd been released, I'd missed the quiet reflections we shared over a cup of watered-down Folgers.

"All right, purge. I want to know it all. Like why Keagan looks like you stole his brain, why your ex is anything but your ex, and why your friend, and I mean that in loose terms, is living your life?" She pulled the sugar bowl toward her and scooped three heaping teaspoons into her cup.

I stalled, searching for a comfortable position and the right words.

She scooted back in her chair and crossed her arms. If this were a real interrogation, her intimidation factor was non-existent. She was going to have to up her game.

"Is this the chair?" Mickey had described her father sitting her down in the confession chair and squeezing out the truth.

She looked at me, confused, then registered my meaning. She nodded and said, "I'm waiting."

I wanted to laugh so badly, but that would have been disrespectful. She had opened her life and home to me, and I would give her the truth.

"You heard it last night. He's a pathological liar and a serial cheater. As for Carla…I don't know what to think. She was supposed to be my friend. My trust was placed in the wrong hands." Carla baffled me. My ability to judge character was impaired. I was zero-for-two.

"I wish we could have been there for you. Your life changed, and no one noticed. You never acted like anything was different." Her voice sounded flat, like somehow I had let her down by not being honest.

"I know, but I didn't have the heart to take the fantasy away from anyone. You were all getting such joy from planning my future."

Rubbing her chin, she looked up as if the answers were written on the ceiling.

She lowered her head and raised her voice. "God, Holly, you could have said something."

"Oh Lord, coulda, woulda, shoulda. It seemed like the best way to go at the time."

"All right." She reached across the table and grasped my hands. "I can't harangue you for keeping an asshole around when I did the same thing myself. It's funny how we make the wrong decisions for what we think are the right reasons."

"Live and learn, right? The truth is, I've had a lot of practice swallowing my tears. So keeping it to myself wasn't such a burden."

Sadness flooded Mickey's expression. She brushed a rogue tear against her shoulder. Her grip on my hands tightened. "But to get fucked over by your fiancé and your best friend..." Mickey released me and pounded her fist on the table. "Screw Carla and the doctor she rode in on." She laughed as the shock waves traveled across the surface and rippled through my coffee.

My mom had always said a small change could make a big ripple. I wondered what a big change would make. I didn't need another wave to knock me off my feet. Prison was enough. Carla seemed like a small disruption when I compared her to everything else.

"If I were you, I'd be enjoying some target practice about now. So...how much did you hate prison anyway?" She rolled her shoulders like a fighter loosening up before he entered the ring. "Should I hide my gun?"

"I'm never going back to prison. I like fresh coffee and hamburgers way too much. Besides, I'm an awful shot." I pulled the sugar toward me and scooped a teaspoon into my mug. I wasn't feeling so sweet and thought the extra serving could help. "You know what pisses me off the most?"

"You only have one thing?"

"I'm pissed my Jeep had over twenty thousand miles put on it while I was away. Thank God it still looks good. If she had damaged my car, I'd be borrowing your gun."

"On second thought, I'm not sure Kerrick would like me to be an accessory to murder. Maybe it's best I keep it under lock and key."

"Probably a good plan. I've already heard the speech about how what I do affects everyone. I can't see murder being overlooked by the McKinleys."

Mickey's mouth opened. "Who told you that? Keagan?" She rose from the table and headed to the door.

I pulled her back. "Stop. Do you want to erase any of the forward movement I've managed to make with that man?" When she settled down, I took our cups to the kitchen and topped them off.

"No, but he had no right to speak for me. What's going on with you two anyway? Yesterday, he was uncharacteristically disengaged —I would say he was rude to you—and today I see him walking you to my door and giving you a kiss on the cheek. What the hell was that about?"

I wished I could shed some light on Keagan. I had no idea what his deal was. "Honestly, I was convinced he hated me. Is he bipolar?"

"I don't think so. He's actually the sweetest of the brothers I know. He's always there to lend a hand. He's never let me down. He may not say the right thing all the time, but he always does the right thing."

"I think he's trying to make up for being disagreeable. He invited me to dinner tonight. He's barbecuing, and I'm bringing dessert."

"Watch out, or you might be dessert. The McKinley boys are hard to resist." She closed her eyes and licked her lips like she was savoring a memory.

"I'm bringing cake. I'm not on the menu, but maybe someday." There was something I saw in Keagan today I wanted to know better. There was a softness that had the potential to heal my cracked heart.

"Don't say I didn't warn you. The McKinleys have a way of getting under your skin, or is that your clothing? I'm not sure, but either way, it could be worth investigating."

"So...if something transpired between Keagan and I, would it be okay with you?" I felt like I was sixteen and asking my mom's permission to go on my first date.

"Total seal of approval. Just don't break each other's hearts. I love you both and couldn't take sides." She sipped her coffee and shivered. Out came the spoon, and in went another scoop of sugar.

"Haven't there been enough broken hearts to last a lifetime?" I settled back in my chair and folded my arms like armor across my chest.

She picked up her cup and sipped at her coffee, studying me over the rim. "What aren't you telling me?"

Mickey didn't get information using intimidation tactics; she used guilt. I wondered if she had put something in the coffee. It seemed like most of our confessions happened over a cup of joe.

I lowered my head in embarrassment. I hemmed and hawed. My next sentence came out in a whisper. "I need Carla and Matt to get my license back."

"What? No fucking way. You're not asking them. That's like going to hell and asking for water." She had risen from her chair and hovered over me.

Stunned by her passionate response, I shrank in my seat and pondered her statement.

"I don't have any options. I met with the board today. I need character references, and Matt and Carla are the people who know me best. I'm asking them."

"I'll write you a damn letter." Her loyalty was fierce.

"I'm touched, but a letter from an ex-convict won't go very far."

Anger surged through her faster than a lightning bolt. She pushed from the table and stepped to the door, opening it and pointing out the door.

"What?" I looked at the door confused.

"Freedom has damaged your brain. Come back when you're

thinking clearly." She leaned against the doorjamb and shook her head. "How much more will you allow them to take from you?"

"I don't have anything else to give either of them." It was the truth. "I imagine Carla's done taking what's mine." If she wanted my life right now, I would have given it to her. I was a mess of uncertainty.

"I get that you need something from them, and they owe you, but they aren't going to pay up. I figured you'd learned not to trust people in prison." Her matter-of-fact tone left no room for discussion.

"I'm asking them. You may not agree, but I have limited resources, and I need to do what I have to do."

I wasn't sure if she would hug me or hit me as I walked toward the door, but she grabbed me and pulled me to her chest before I walked through. She appeared more concerned than angry.

"Don't come crying to me when it all goes to shit." She let me loose and closed the door before I could respond.

She gave me a lot to think about. I left with more questions than when I'd arrived. Was I making a mistake by counting on Carla and Matt to do the right thing? Didn't I owe my trust and loyalty to Mickey? She'd never let me down. Maybe the only one to consider was myself, and what I'd wanted. When was the last time I'd put my needs first?

Chapter 9

HOLLY

I ground a path in the entry waiting for five o'clock to arrive. My living room had appeared lifeless yesterday but seemed to be gaining warmth. Perspective and some pretty purple flowers changed everything.

The minute hand bobbled before it clicked into place. I scooped up the cake and my jacket and headed out the door.

Once I dashed across the gravel walkway, I was one hand short for a proper knock. I tapped the tip of my boot on the lower panel of the wooden door. *Thunk. Thunk. Thunk.*

"Coming."

Keagan swung the door open, and my jaw nearly hit the porch. Dressed in jeans and nothing but a white towel draped around his neck, this man had it going on. A single stream of water dripped from his wet hair, rolled down his face, and dropped to the center of his chest, disappearing into the curly wisps of dark hair.

I snapped my mouth shut. "I can come back later." My voice squeaked. It had been a long time since I'd seen a man's bare chest. I could have stood there all night and watched the water evaporate from his skin. It was taking a bit of self-restraint not to lick him dry.

"No way." He stepped aside. "Come on in." He pulled the towel from his neck, and my heart skipped a beat. Tight, sinewy muscles stretched from shoulder to shoulder. "I didn't want to smell like a barn when you came over."

He looked at my full hands, pulled my jacket from my arm, and tossed it on the pine table near the front door. A twist of his torso caused his muscles to bunch, each one honed to perfection.

"You smell like pine." I cringed. Here I was standing in this gorgeous man's home, and all I could say was *you smell like pine*. Trying to up my intelligence quotient, I added, "Fresh and outdoorsy." If anything, I'd proven I could hold my own in a conversation with any kindergarten student around.

"Thanks. You smell good, too. Sweet." He leaned in toward me and breathed deeply. "Mmm." He made the same sound I made when something smelled delicious.

"That good, huh? Maybe it's the cake you smell, and not me." I hoped it was me he smelled. I'd showered and shaved and slathered my body in coconut and mango lotion.

He glanced at the cake in my hands. "Why don't you put it in the kitchen, and by the way, that cake has nothin' on you, darlin'." He pointed me to a kitchen that looked exactly like mine. He licked his lips like he was tasting the air, then turned around and walked away. "I'll be right out."

I walked backward, giving him a once over as he walked down the hallway and turned into the first bedroom, the same room that would have been mine if our houses were flipped.

I slid the cake onto the counter. I'd imagined the typical bachelor pad, but this wasn't anywhere close. He had a fruit bowl in the center of his table. He was completely domesticated.

The layout of his furniture was slightly different from mine. His sofa faced the television, whereas mine kept the fireplace as the focal point. Large and small pictures lined the wooden beam of his mantel. I was drawn to the pictures. Beautiful people surrounded him at various moments in his life.

Kerrick and Killian were easily recognized. An older version of Kerrick stood with his arms draped over Keagan's shoulders. In

Set Aside

their hands was an enormous trophy. I couldn't make out the words, but ribbons draped the horse behind him.

Next was a picture of a woman with a baby. I picked it up and studied it. The woman looked happy. The baby was a boy if his blue clothes were any indication to his sex. It had to be Keagan. Even then, his blue-sky-meets-the-green-sea eyes were unique in every way. His little fingers gripped a wooden toy horse. I was mesmerized by the photo of him locked lovingly in the arms of his stunning young mother.

"I was six months old in that photo."

I all but jumped out of my skin, then swung around. "Oh."

He grinned at my jumpiness, or maybe my nervousness, or just his memory of his mother. I couldn't tell. I couldn't figure Keagan out.

"Even then, I loved horses. I bet your baby pictures have a stethoscope wrapped around your neck." He took the picture from my hands and placed it back on the mantel.

"Nope. Don't have any baby pictures."

He looked at me as if I'd just told him I'd been hatched from an egg, which was altogether a possibility. Prior to five, I hadn't existed.

I shook my head. He would never understand. "It's a long story for another day."

"Okay." His confused look slid away. "Are you starving, or can you hold off for an hour?"

"I won't waste away in an hour. Why?"

He took my hand and steered me toward the door. When he helped me into my jacket, I was surprised. Chivalry wasn't dead, but when it came to Keagan, it was not always present. This was a nice change.

"You haven't had an opportunity to tour the ranch." He hopped across the floor as he tugged on his boots. "I thought I'd take you on a short ride."

"The last time I rode was about ten years ago, maybe longer." I stalled on the edge of the porch. "I'm not sure I could control a horse on my own."

"We'll go slow." He guided me behind our cabins to the stables, where two horses were saddled and ready to go. He'd given this moment thought. Planned. Prepared. "Why did you stop riding?"

"Life got in the way." Horseback riding had been a treat in the early days. "Mom worked a lot, and money was tight." I treasured the memories where she and I hung out together and looked after one another. She was really good at the looking after part. I had failed miserably.

"It's like riding a bike; it'll come back to you." Keagan clucked, and both horses looked at him. "We'll have you back in the saddle in no time. Tonight, we'll ride together." The darker, almost black horse snorted and came forward.

"This guy here is Brody." Keagan ruffled the big horse's head. "He's the super stud of the ranch." A lighter brown horse pushed his muzzle into Keagan's chest. "This young man is Diesel." He reached out and tugged on the horse's mane. "He's doing his best to keep up with the super stud. He fathered one of the foals we're expecting next year."

"You lied to me." I kept my voice teasing, but still, his brows rose. "You aren't the ranch's master breeder. Brody is, and Diesel runs a close second. That means you're back in third place."

"Yeah, well I seem to fall comfortably in third." His tone was resigned, and something glinted across his face. I wasn't sure if it was irritation or disappointment. It certainly hadn't resembled humor. "But that's a subject for another day."

Touché.

"Another day sounds promising." Quite honestly, I was intrigued. Call me crazy, but I was attracted to many facets of this man. Like me, I felt he was misunderstood. He tried to push off his aloofness as independence, but I recognized loneliness.

Keagan jumped the fence in one fluid movement. "We only have about forty minutes of daylight left." With speed and efficiency, he removed the saddle from Diesel and set him free to run within the confines of the paddock.

"Let's get crackin', then." I eyed the big horse. He looked strong, but... "Can Brody handle our combined weight?"

"Brody will have no problem handling both of us. Besides, you don't weigh that much." He helped me mount the big black stallion. When he swung up behind me, his solid thighs pressed against me, and for a second I wondered what it would feel like to be pressed under his naked body.

The slightest shake of the reins had us moving in the direction of the open pasture. I was trapped between the saddle horn and him, and I couldn't decide what was the lesser of two evils. The jarring movements made the horn vibrate against me, causing sensations I hadn't felt in a long time. His hard body pressed against me had my mind wishing this was something more.

"Are you comfortable?" The reins slackened in his hand, giving Brody permission to lead the way while his arms slid around my waist.

"Um...yeah." 'Comfortable' wasn't the word I'd have used to describe what I was feeling. Aroused. Stimulated. Horny.

He pulled me back against him. "Relax and enjoy." He pressed his hand against my stomach.

I had no choice but to lean into him. My head fit like perfection under his chin. My body relaxed against his firm chest. This kind of comfort had never been mine. I wanted this.

The setting sun created a pale pumpkin sky. Tall blades of last year's grass softened the spiky fronds of the yucca plants that dotted the countryside.

"Mickey's land runs the length of this trail all the way to the top of that hill." I followed his point to a mountain he described as a hill, but who was I to argue? "I thought we would ride to the top and watch the sun sink behind Pikes Peak. Is that okay with you?"

"Mmm hmm."

It's not like I had much choice. I was trapped between him and the saddle horn. If he had told me we were trotting to Los Angeles on horseback, I would have been game.

"I go there when I need to think." He dipped his lips to my ear, and his breath whispered across my neck. Goosebumps skittled down my chest. "It's a special place, Holly."

I stiffened. Felt like he was talking about more than a place. "Why?" My voice croaked, and I swallowed hard. "I thought you didn't like me?" I'd learned in prison that nice usually came with a price, and I wondered if I could afford Keagan.

"Holly," he sighed against my hair, "I'm going to be honest with you, but more importantly, I'm going to be honest with myself." His arm tightened around my waist.

My natural inclination was to lean in to his chest and give myself over to him.

"You're a distraction."

His words went bone deep. "A good distraction, or a bad one?"

"The jury is out. All I know is you hopped out of Mickey's truck, and shit changed." He tugged the reins to the left, and our direction changed.

"I thought you hated me because I had a criminal record." He pinned me in place when I twisted. To see his face when he spoke would have been nice. I was better at reading expressions than I was at reading tone.

"Your criminal record is the least attractive thing about you. That, and your taste in men." I wondered if he realized he'd put himself down. "I was an ass. I'm sorry. I should have treated you better. Mickey's word is gold. She said you were a wonderful person, and I should have believed her. You've given me no reason to believe you're anything short of amazing."

The last time someone called me amazing was the day I left my mom for good. She had grabbed my face between her cold palms and told me never to forget how amazing I was. I never thought I'd hear someone utter those words to me again.

Keagan jumped off the horse first. I was still stuck on *amazing* and didn't realize we'd stopped. With his help, I slipped off the side of Brody and into Keagan's arms.

He turned me around, and I gazed upon the most incredible sunset I'd ever seen. The sky was painted in orange, red, and yellow. The mountains appeared purple against the backdrop. The world had silenced itself to let me enjoy this view without distraction. Well, almost without distraction. Keagan slid up behind me, and my mind turned to goo.

"Oh, wow." Words escaped me.

"'Wow' hardly covers it." His arms wrapped around my waist, and his chin rested on my head. "That's how I felt yesterday when I saw you."

My heart stilled. Colors splashed the sky. I finally understood. "So you were the little boy on the playground who punched the girl he liked right before he kissed her?"

He spun me around. His eyes went on forever.

My heart thudded against my ribs.

"Yes."

He pressed his lips against mine. His tongue probed and prodded, demanding access I readily gave. One hand smoothed down my back and came to rest on the curve of my bottom.

He took his time.

I savored the kiss.

My knees buckled.

He pulled me possessively against his body.

Desire flooded my senses. I'd never felt so raw and exposed by a simple kiss. The problem was, it wasn't a simple kiss. He'd branded me, and I would feel him on my lips forever.

With a final stroke of his tongue, he pulled away and looked at me with an expression that resembled awe. I was positive my expression mirrored his.

I couldn't explain how I felt; I was an amalgamation of lust and fear and hope. The moment turned awkward while I stared at him in silence. I twisted around to watch the sun drop behind Pikes Peak. When the final ray sank behind the snowcapped peak, he helped me mount Brody and swung up behind me.

I leaned in to him. "Can we do this again?" I whispered. I wasn't positive I wanted him to answer. How would I feel if he said no?

"The ride, or the kiss?" His voice contained a touch of humor.

"Both." Today had been my best day in two years. I wanted more. I needed more. After all the shit I'd been through, all I'd lost, I wanted this, even if it was just for the moment. I had a feeling he would be worth the risk.

"How hungry are you?" His hand slid around my body, grazing my breast. My nipples sprung to attention, reaching for his touch.

How did I answer when my hunger for him seemed to have swallowed my hunger for food? I answered honestly. "I'm famished...for intimacy. Food can wait."

With a cluck and a shake of the reins, Brody's walk turned into a trot. We made it to the cabins in half the time it had taken us to get up the hill.

I dropped from the horse into Keagan's arms. "I need to take care of Brody, but I'll hurry. Go inside and make yourself comfortable." He leaned down and gave me a kiss.

I turned around and walked toward his cabin like a schoolgirl in a daze. But I was not a schoolgirl. I was a woman. A woman who savored the moisture he left on my lips.

And like any other twenty-seven-year-old woman, I had needs. Wasn't it time those needs were met?

Chapter 10

KEAGAN

"Brody, you're getting cheated today." I carefully removed his saddle. I was in a rush, and Brody might not get any extras, but he would get the essentials. I was never one to skimp on the important details. "No brush down, no extra treats." I moved him into the enclosure. "I've got a beautiful filly waiting for me inside. You understand, right?"

He vocalized his discontent with a loud snort, then walked away, showing me his big ole ass.

"Same to you, buddy."

I headed straight for the house. Kicked off my boots the second my feet hit the porch. Stalled at the closed door. The silent house made me nervous in a way I hadn't expected. Did she get cold feet and head to her cabin? I walked quietly across the floor.

She stood in the closet of my bedroom. I'd never caught a girl snooping through my clothes. They've rummaged through my drawers and rifled through my wallet, but this was a first for me.

She pulled my denim jacket to her nose and inhaled. The action, although odd, was incredibly sexy, especially when she sighed.

"Better than horse shit, right?"

She jumped. The squeak she made was cute.

"How did you sneak up on me?"

She dropped the sleeve of my jacket but wouldn't look at me. She crossed the room, but I didn't get out of her way.

"No boots." I pulled her into my arms. "After getting Mama's wooden spoon, I learned." She smelled so good. Felt even better.

"What else did your mom teach you?"

Her hands ran up my chest, and I shuddered. Her touch did crazy shit to my body. My dick stood at attention.

"Everything I'm going to do to you and with you is self-taught."

Her face lit up. Her huge smile reached her eyes. I'd be damned if my heart didn't nearly explode. If I could bring laughter to her eyes every day, I'd consider myself a happy man.

How did I end up whipped in less than a day? I couldn't blame it on the space between her legs, because I hadn't settled myself there yet.

I took her to my bed.

Trembling, she looked at the door as if ready to bolt.

"Don't be nervous." The mattress sagged under my weight. With a tug, I pulled her onto my chest.

Her heart hummingbirded. "Nervous doesn't begin to describe what I'm feeling. Desperate and scared shitless is more like it."

I held her tighter. Distraction; she needed a distraction. She reminded me of a stallion that hadn't been broken.

"Kiss me." I kept my words at a whisper, and she shivered as if uncertain I was friend or foe. The best way to train a wild one was to prove myself trustworthy.

Slow and steady, I pulled her up my body so I could reach her mouth. An involuntary groan escaped from me as our parts rubbed together. Her sweet lips tentatively touched mine and grew more confident. Every muscle of my body was stretched tight with want, but I refused to rush her.

Her lips pulled from mine. "What if I'm not enough?" Her baby blues stared into my eyes with a vulnerability I could feel.

How could this beautiful woman not be enough? Her uncertainty gripped my heart. Was it because she felt unworthy? Or was it

Set Aside

because we were moving like a freight train through a farmhouse? Too fast? Too soon?

She drew several breaths past her kiss-swollen lips. Her cheeks were pink and flushed, which was a good look on her.

"Let's slow down." I traced her lips with my finger. "I don't want you to feel uncomfortable, and I certainly don't want you to ever think you're not enough." Her eyes were full of questions. "I want the things we do to be epic. Maybe we should ratchet this back a step. Hell, I don't even know your last name." She needed more than a quick roll in my bed.

"McGrath, my full name is Holly Maria McGrath." She gushed her answer in an exhale.

"Well, Holly Maria McGrath, that's a good Irish name." I brushed the hair from her face, trying to see her eyes. "You're already perfect in my book. In fact, being Irish puts you in the top tier."

The passion in her eyes dimmed. "Better knock me down a few steps." Her voice softened. "I'm Irish by name only. I have no idea what my real ethnicity is. I was abandoned at birth by a teenage mother."

Holy shit. Never expected that. The way this girl loved the memory of her mother was fierce. Her confession cleared up one thing: the reason she had no baby pictures.

"You are Irish. I'm sure your mom beat our Irish values into you all the time. Hell, most people are Irish one day a year, and if I have my way, I'll put a little Irish in you every day."

She may have thought I was joking, but once I sank myself inside her, I knew that would be where I'd always want to be.

"What's your full name?" She ran her free hand through my hair, making my scalp tingle where she touched.

In my best Irish accent, I answered her. "I'm Keagan Braden McKinley, the third child of Kathryn and Kane McKinley."

"Nice accent." Her hand stroked the prickly whiskers on my face. I elaborated simply to keep her eyes on me. I wasn't ready to lose this connection.

"My ancestors hail from County Kildare. I come from a long

line of horse thieves." I never would have made it as an Irish narrator, but I laughed at how silly she made me feel. Silly felt good.

Holly grabbed a chunk of my cheek and tugged it back and forth. "And you were judging me because I'm an ex-convict?" Her voiced filled with humor-laced indignation. Yep, she could pass for Irish.

"Nationality was never important to me. All I wanted was for my woman to be a paragon of virtue, but in hindsight that would never work. She has to hold her ground in the McKinley family, and that will require a bit of backbone and a wild streak."

Her leg rose up to hook around my hip. The heel of her boot pulled against me until we were touching thigh to thigh.

"You can't possibly have boots on in my bed. My mother would have knocked you upside the head for that sin."

I slid from her body and pulled off her boots. Her slim feet were covered in cat socks; not the type of pussy I'd hoped to see tonight.

"Your mother sounds like mine—strict. I was able to wear shoes in the house, but the utterance of a cuss word, and I was blowing bubbles from my mouth for days." Her nose curled into a look of disgust. "It wasn't until jail that I finally used the words 'shit' and 'asshole'. I'll never be comfortable using the F-word you cowboys and Mickey toss around like leftover pennies." Wrapping her legs around my waist, she pulled me back to the bed. I happily accommodated her wishes.

"It's just a word that seems to hold power over people. It depends on how you use it. For example, if I said I wanted to fuck you over, and if my voice contained malice, it would mean a totally different thing than if I said I wanted to fuck you over my kitchen counter." I gave her a sideways glance, not sure how she would take my example.

Her lips fell open, and I slipped her a kiss. Our tongues danced together. She tasted so sweet. She pressed her body forward, and I wondered if I should pull back. My brain said slow down, my dick said full speed ahead; my dick won.

Out of habit, my hands began to roam. Her button-down shirt fell open, leaving me with a vision so heavenly, I questioned if I were still alive. Rounded globes threatened to spill from her lace bra. The tips of her nipples pressed against the material. I popped the front enclosure and set them free. Perfect ivory skin blended into her pink rosebuds.

"Oh my God," she moaned as I plucked one tight bud into my mouth. Its hardness could rival my own. Once again, I lifted and shifted, trying to find a less constricting position.

"Fuck, you have perfect breasts." I wanted to smack myself for blurting that out. What was I, twelve?

"Used in that context fuck is a very sexy word." She panted for breath and dug her claws into the back of my shirt.

"You're sexy. You're so damn sexy," I mumbled against her soft creamy skin.

"I don't feel sexy."

Brakes. I slammed on the brakes. "Who told you you weren't sexy? Matt?" How could this woman not feel sexy? My raging hard-on was pressed into her thigh, but I had more to think about than my pleasure. "He's an asshole, and you deserve better." I was better. She deserved me. The talk of Matt had shriveled my desire. I rolled onto my back and stared at the ceiling.

"I'll never go back to him." She scooted to the edge of the bed and buttoned up her shirt. "I settled then, but I'll never settle again." Our moment had passed, and I wasn't going to push. This little gal deserved respect.

The mattress sprang up as I hopped off the bed and pulled her into my arms. Held close to my chest, I brushed my lips against her silky hair. She smelled like wildflowers and coconut.

I wanted to punch the living daylights out of Matt for having taken so much from this woman. She was a delicate flower that needed to grow a few thorns.

"Let's eat."

I tugged at her hand and pulled her toward the kitchen. Instead of lighting up the BBQ, I decided to pan fry the burgers. It was the quickest way to get food into her grumbling stomach.

With potato salad and burger filled plates, we plopped on the sofa and turned on the TV. I scrolled through the channels until I landed on the Hallmark channel. What could I say? I had a thing for romance.

"This is my second burger in as many days, but I have to say this is the best yet."

A dribble of juice ran down her chin, but she caught it with her tongue before it got too far. There was so much I could imagine when it came to her tongue. I needed to control my thoughts, so I edged away from her to gain distance. If I weren't careful, I'd lose my tightly coiled self-restraint and she'd be under my body again.

"Out of prison for two days, and all we feed you are burgers. I could have made something else." A new movie was just starting. The title was *A Chance at Romance;* it seemed fitting for the moment.

"You really want to watch a Hallmark movie with me?"

"Yes. I used to watch them just to laugh at how silly they were, but I think I may be a romantic."

She focused her attention on her meal. Just when I thought our conversation was dead, she asked, "If you're such a romantic, why don't you have a wife or a girlfriend?"

I turned down the volume so I could concentrate on her. "I've been told I have until I'm thirty-five before women start thinking I'm damaged or too set in my ways. At twenty-eight, I still have time." I reached over and brushed off the catsup that pooled in the corner of her lip. "I've been focusing the things I considered more important—my education, my reputation, and my career."

"I feel the same way about my nursing license. I worked too hard to let it slip away from me." She put her empty plate on the coffee table.

I'd never seen a woman inhale a meal so quickly. "What if you can't get your license back?" I hated to hit her upside the head with reality, but having a felony conviction was going to limit her options.

"That's like me asking you what you'd do if you couldn't breed horses." She was pissed all the way from the glare in her eyes to the arms that folded defiantly over her chest.

She had a point. When a person worked their entire life to achieve one thing and that one thing got ripped out from under them, what was left?

Set Aside

"I get it, but you have to consider something other than nursing in case it doesn't go your way." With a gentle hand, I caressed the top of her leg. "If I couldn't breed horses, I'd do something around horses. My options aren't limited to breeding. Yours aren't limited to nursing. Keep an open mind."

"I can't think about it. I thought going to prison was bad, but this is worse. At least in prison I didn't have to hope to be anything but a convict. Now that I'm out, I may never get past my sentence." Her head fell low, and she looked at everything but me.

"Look at me." She wasn't going to hide from me. I lifted her chin so she had to look in my eyes. "Something happened today that you're not sharing. Tell me what's bothering you."

"At my meeting today, they said I'd need several letters—three, to be exact—all from peers that can attest to my professional skills and personal conduct." She scooted in closer to me. "Matt and Carla are the only two people I know well enough to ask. In the two years I've been gone, I've lost many contacts. I feel like I'm on this endless free fall." She leaned into my side, and I was happy to give her the comfort she needed. I would be her safe place to land.

"Holly, I'm begging you to remove them from your list. Carla isn't a friend, and Matt would want something in return. Go to the hospital and see who's still there before you ask them."

"You sound like Mickey, and I'll tell you the same thing I told her: I'm asking them. They owe me." Her tone brooked no argument.

They owed her for sure, but she'd never get the payback she deserved. I could see it clearly. She couldn't, and that frustrated me. I had to separate myself from the situation. I let out an exasperated exhale and stood up.

I tossed our dishes into the bubbly water and watched them sink out of sight, something I wanted Carla and Matt to do. I hoped she would reconsider. She didn't hear the things Matt wanted to do to her. I did. Hell, I wanted to do them myself, but I wasn't going to swizzle my stick in every nurse at the hospital, just the one living next door to me. Once I was in, I was all in.

When I returned to the couch, she was sifting through the channels. The room was cloaked in darkness except for the glow coming from the television.

"What about *Orange is the New Black*?" she asked. It surprised me she wanted to watch a show about women prisoners, but I was game. Maybe it would give me some insight into her life.

"Won't that be like watching the Biography Channel?"

I slipped in next to her and pulled her to me. I couldn't get close enough. I wanted to hug her and kiss her, but I'd settle for holding her. We sat in silence and watched an episode where all of the carrots and cucumbers had disappeared from the kitchen. I pondered the scene for a few minutes.

"So women really do that?"

She leaned back and looked at me. "You really want to know about the sex lives of inmates?" As if her words weren't enough, she mimed the universal sign for sex: index finger stroking into the closed palm of her hand.

"Hell yeah." I wanted to know.

"Okay, but it's bad. Remember, I worked in the kitchen." She tilted her head and bugged out her eyes. "Some women will use anything they can to simulate a man's part. They even roll feminine hygiene pads into tubes and shove them into latex gloves or sandwich bags. That's fine unless you're allergic to latex; then you get a rash that will rival the clap."

"Really? I thought they did the lady-lovin' thing." Her expression gave nothing away.

"Some do, but most try to self-gratify." She leaned back against me. "One girl who worked in the kitchen traded cucumbers and carrots for cigarettes." She burst out laughing.

"Was that you?" I reached down and tried to tickle her, but she swatted my hand away.

"Nope, but I'm a nurse, and people came to me when they didn't want to wait in the infirmary. What I saw could make any woman want to avoid rubber and phallic vegetables." Laughter bubbled out of her, forcing her to bend in half.

"Details." Would she give me some? I was a guy, and this shit was fascinating.

She sat up, clutching her stomach. "Use your imagination. And remember, anything is possible. Women in prison can be resourceful." She flipped through the channel and settled on *American Idol*.

"That's it? That's all you're giving me? What about you?" I dared to ask.

"I guess I waited for you." She snuggled in closer and wrapped her hands around my waist.

"I'm glad you did. I'll make sure I'm worthy of you." We shared a long, hot kiss before turning back to the TV.

Movies and music became our neutral topic, along with food and hobbies. She liked to read. I liked to do Sudoku puzzles. She preferred red meat to anything else. I was right with her on that. She loved irises. I couldn't tell the difference between an iris and a petunia. By the end of the evening, I felt like I knew her—really knew her. I liked her—really liked her.

"What's on your schedule tomorrow?"

The last time a girl asked me a question about my schedule, I was in college and she was trying to squeeze into one of my open slots. Actually, she was trying to get me to squeeze into one of hers; it wasn't much of a squeeze.

"We have a new ranch hand moving onto the property tomorrow." I didn't know how I felt about a stranger living next to Holly. "The stables are full, and Killian and I could use the help. He'll be a good fit."

"Does Mickey make enough to pay you and hire a couple others? I feel bad about taking one of her cabins. She could be renting mine out." She tensed in my arms. She stiffened from her shoulders to her hips. Her once pliant body turned to stone.

"She saved cabins for all you girls." I shifted so we were lying on the couch, her in front of me. "We have twenty-one paid boarders and profitable grazing land." When she scooted her bottom against me, I groaned. She giggled. She was killing me.

"I can't imagine having to deal with this ranch alone." She pulled the hand I'd placed on her hip over her body and tugged me close.

I pressed myself firmly to her backside. What was I going to do with this woman? A little voice crawled inside my head and told me, *Love her.*

"She wasn't alone. She had Kerrick. Kerrick had us. Now you have us, so you will never be alone again." I spun her around, and she gripped me like a buoy in deep water. She clung to me, not Matt. "What about you? What's on your agenda?" All I could think about was seeing her again.

"I'll visit the cemetery in the morning, then go to the hospice that took care of my mom in her final days. After that, I'm going to the hospital to track down some letters." She rolled herself away and into an upright position.

The air around me chilled from her absence. A glance at the clock showed we had talked for hours. I wanted to keep her here all night, but I knew I should get her home.

"How about dinner tomorrow?"

"How about I make it?"

"That sounds even better. I'll bring the dessert. I have a delicious chocolate cake we never ate."

"That's cheating." She poked me in the chest. "But it's the kind I can overlook."

"I've never been a cheater." I looked into her eyes and hoped she saw my sincerity. "For the record, I would have waited for you."

Her expression turned soft. Holly needed to be needed, and I understood that about her. For a brief moment, I thought she might cry.

I swooped in and closed my mouth over hers. I didn't want her to shed another tear for that asshole.

Breathless, she pulled away. "For the record, I typically don't fall into a guy's bed the second day I know him." She gently palmed my cheek before she rose and started for the door. "It's been a long time; besides, you might be the best kisser I've ever kissed." She turned to face me. "Except, of course, for Helen from laundry at the prison."

Helen?

Her eyes gave nothing away, but the twitch of her lip finally gave in to laughter.

"Did you really kiss a woman named Helen while you were locked up?" I couldn't see my Holly making out with some woman named Helen. *My Holly? Wow.*

"Oh yeah, Helen had a thing for me. One day she laid a wet, juicy kiss on me. Thank God I ended up in the kitchen instead of laundry." Her eyes lifted like she was remembering something. "On occasion, I'd find hearts drawn on my underwear. Kind of a sweet gesture, don't you think?"

It took seconds to stalk her to the door. "You compared me with Helen, the wet, sloppy kisser? I'm wounded." I showed her how sloppy a kiss could really be. Pride filled me as her tongue swept across her swollen red lips to lick off the extra moisture I'd left behind. "Let's get you home."

Reluctantly, I helped her with her boots and walked her across to her cabin. The moonlight cast a glow on the pumpkins lined up on her porch. I wondered why she needed so many.

As if reading my mind, she said, "We're having a pumpkin carving contest, and I aim to win." She opened her door and looked at me like she was debating if she should invite me in or not. In the end, she stepped aside and I walked in.

"When are we having this contest?" I glanced around her place. "I'll have you know I watch *The Food Network* religiously. I'll not have you count me out just yet." It didn't have a lived-in look yet, but it was on its way. There were flowers and photos that made it seem homey.

"Soon. I have to ask Mickey when she's free." She kicked off her boots and tossed them toward the door. Quick Learner. "Obviously before Halloween. *The Food Network? Hallmark?* Who the heck are you?"

"I'm the guy who's going to tuck you in and kiss you goodnight. Go brush your teeth and slip on your night clothes." I yanked off my boots out of habit and walked toward her.

She smiled up at me in childlike wonder. She was a grown, beautiful child with the nicest set of breasts known to man. I kissed her, turned her toward the hallway, and swatted her perfect ass lightly.

The water running in the bathroom could be heard throughout the house. I wondered if she realized I'd heard her cry all night long. She had to be exhausted.

While I waited, I picked up the pictures from the mantel. She was right, no baby photos. The oldest one showed a little girl around five, picking white flowers from a bush. A stocky woman with dark hair smiled behind her. I scanned the pictures. It was like watching a slide show of Holly growing up. Always present was the smiling dark-haired woman.

"That was my mom." Holly leaned against the mantel in front of me, dressed in nothing but a long T-shirt. "Her name was Connie, and that was her prize gardenia bush. It was quite a boon for a single thirty-five-year-old woman to adopt a child. I'd been shuffled through the system for years, and she thought I'd had enough. The twenty-two years we had together weren't nearly enough."

"There's never enough time." Emotion clouded her eyes. "Did you ever notice how your mom's eyes smiled when she did? Yours do, too. I love that about you. It's easy to tell when you're being authentic, and when you're putting on a brave face. Last night, I saw your brave face. Today, I saw you."

With my hand on the small of her back, I walked her to her room. I knew exactly which one she used. It was directly across from mine.

She climbed into bed after I folded the soft cover back. I caught a glimpse of her thigh as she slid down and her Red Hot Chili Peppers T-shirt slid up. I looked away for my sake, not hers.

Flowers scented the air, but there weren't any about. The candle on her nightstand sat with an unburned wick.

"I want to stay until you fall asleep." She wasn't alone, and I wanted her to fall asleep knowing that. Another repeat of last night would crush me.

"Sweet, but a bit weird, don't you think?"

My weight sank into the mattress beside her. Her body rolled into me.

With a heavy sigh, I confessed. "I heard you crying last night."

Her eyes went wide. "I don't want you to ever feel alone again. Even if it means I sit here every night until you fall asleep." It wasn't immediately clear how she felt. I only knew how I felt, and it was unlike anything I'd experienced before.

"Oh, my gosh, how embarrassing. I was thinking about my mom, and Carla, and Matt, and then you were so mean to me. It was overwhelming. I'm sorry I kept you up."

"Holly, stop." Her apology was not what I'd wanted. "I'm sorry I was mean to you. I was feeling things I didn't know how to handle, things that caught me off guard. I promise you will never cry because of me again."

She was silent.

I focused on the nightstand. "How about we light this candle?"

She scooted in closer and nodded. In search of a match, I opened the drawer and got a big shock, and I mean big. Sitting side by side was a jumbo pack of D batteries and the biggest vibrator I'd ever seen.

Holly leaned forward. When her eyes latched onto what I was looking at, she let out a scream. "I'm going to kill Mickey."

Chapter 11

HOLLY

There were three things I wanted when I woke up in the morning. Hot coffee. A kiss from Keagan. And to kill Mickey. I padded into my kitchen to start the coffee. Two out of the three could be reasonably met. The third would take some planning, because I wasn't up for another stint in the slammer.

I stepped onto the wooden porch with two cups of coffee in my hands. Steam rose from the cups of fresh brew and disappeared into the crisp morning air. In the distance, the sun's rays barely kissed the prairie. It would be a beautiful day.

To my left, voices rose. Keagan's loud and clear mixed with a deep voice, vaguely familiar but un-peggable.

When I rounded the corner of the staff stables, I was excited to see Cole, the chocolate cake cowboy. "Hey Cole, so you're the new hand?" I scootched up next to Keagan and handed him the mug of coffee.

"Well, damn girl. I was hoping to see you again, and here you are. Wish granted." He ignored Keagan and picked me up, swinging me around like a cowboy at a hoedown.

"Put me down," I called out in amusement. I glanced at

Keagan, who didn't appear to be as entertained. He stood with balled fists and an angry glare focused on Cole.

"How was that cake?" Cole looked toward me, then Keagan.

"We never got to it. Keagan makes a mean burger, and by the time we were finished with dinner, we were so full we couldn't eat another bite."

Keagan's head tilted, and his eyes half closed. His expression screamed jealousy, and I liked it. It made me feel like I had value. Looking between the two men, I watched to see if fists would fly. No fists, just looks that could curl toenails. The tension was as thick as motor oil.

I leaned comfortably against Keagan and slipped my arm around his waist. He leaned down and gave me a kiss on the cheek; he had marked his territory. I'd never had anyone but my mom choose me for the right reasons, and this felt right.

He stepped in front of me, blocking out Cole. "How'd you sleep?" He searched my eyes for something. The truth?

"I've never slept better." I reached up and pecked him lightly on the cheek. I'd never been an exhibitionist, but I liked claiming Keagan, too.

"Glad to hear it." He turned to Cole and pointed to the stables. Cole turned and headed for Brody's stall.

"Do you have time to take a quick break?" Without a moment's hesitation, he guided me to my cabin. Our coffee cups hit the table, and my lips were on his. "I had to kiss you before I left."

"Why. Does. Cole. Know. About. Our. Cake?" His question came out in a staccato rhythm, with each word broken by a kiss.

I don't know how he could think about Cole when our lips were commingling. I could barely breathe, nonetheless think. He looked at me with eyes the color of a full spectrum sea, and I wondered if they changed with his mood.

"He was at the store, and I asked him to help." I wrapped my arms around Keagan's body and held him tight.

"You won't need his help again." His kisses weren't gentle. They were predatory and demanding. "Are we taking this attraction further, Holly? If so, he's invisible to you." He held my chin and stared into my eyes. He wasn't looking for my answer; he was demanding my obedience. The intensity burned his message into my brain, tattooing my frontal lobe. I belonged to him.

"My lips are on you, and no one else. There's no need for this alpha male chest pounding routine."

"Good." His soft lips brushed gently against mine. "Lying next to you last night gave me a glimpse of what things could be like." The alpha was banked, and in his place was the soft Hallmark Channel man who had the potential to seize my heart. "Forgive me."

"You're forgiven." I laughed at how easy it was to forgive him in spite of my bruised heart and frayed trust. I wanted to stand here all day and kiss him, but he had a ranch to run, and I had a life to recover. "Now go train that man so you have more time for me."

"What's our plan for tonight?" His arms circled me, coming to rest on my bottom before pulling me against his body.

"I haven't planned the whole night." I loved the way our bodies fit together. The way his chest felt under my palms. He had a body honed by hard work. He was hot. Steamin' hot, and I craved his heat. "We'll start with pasta and figure the rest out. Shall we shoot for six?"

"That late?" He winked at me, and I could have fallen into a puddle at his boots.

I needed a bit of distance to get my heart on straight before it fell out of my chest. "I'll see you at six." I pulled open the door. "Should I invite Cole?" It was a poor joke, and I knew it the minute it slipped from my mouth.

He grabbed my arm. "Don't push." He reeled me close. "I don't share well." He punished me with another burning kiss, and I forgot about distance, cowhands, and the doctor who'd thrown me over for my best friend. "I'm serious. I've spent my whole life fighting for my place. Third child, third son, third in breeding on the ranch." He lifted his brows in a challenge. "This time I want to know my place from the onset, and if it's anything short of first, I'm not interested." He walked out the door, then stopped, reversed, and kissed me with enough passion to soak my panties.

In forty-eight hours, this man had rocked my existence.

After a change of clothes and a drive to Franktown, I stopped at the old cemetery and wandered through a hundred years of burials to the recesses of the property. I stopped before Connie Ellen McGrath's simple stone. "Hi, Mom." I pulled the weeds from her grave, as if waiting for her to answer, to tell me what to do. What do you say to the woman who didn't give birth to you, but gave you life?

"Hey, Mom, I'm free. At least my body is; my head is still trapped in the past. I'm working on moving forward, but it's hard without you."

The tombstone stood at attention, as if tentatively listening.

"I think you'd like Keagan. He's a bit of a Neanderthal, but I think his heart is in the right place. He's a cowboy. You're probably laughing at that, but after dating an asshole doctor, he's a refreshing change."

Her voice in my head chastised my use of the word asshole.

"He was an asshole, Mom. There isn't a more fitting word." The taste of soap came to the forefront of my memory. Irish Spring green. Smells great. Tastes awful.

I told her about the betrayal, and how angry I was that we'd both been set aside. Me since birth. Her since her family abandoned her when she decided to raise a child outside of wedlock. Didn't people like us deserve to be happy, to be first at least sometimes?

I could almost hear her smiling. Mom would want that for me. I plucked the last weed from her grave. "I gotta go." I wished I could have hugged her one more time, but the wind carried a whisper of my mother's voice, telling me I needed to move on.

Ten miles down the road, I turned into the winding driveway and pulled in front of a single-story building that looked more like a ranch house than an institutional building. My mother's last home. Large stone pillars flanked the front door. Were the pillars simply decoration, or did they support the weight of the sorrow that filled the building?

After several minutes of hiding in my Jeep, I swallowed the bile that burned my throat and stepped onto the crushed stone path. It was time to face my fears.

On the front porch, my knuckles turned white from my grip on the door handle. I would never forgive myself if she died in an awful place. I dropped my hand and paced the wooden porch. Potted plants sat between comfortable looking benches. The scent of flowers filled the air while a rainbow of color cascaded over the massive cement planters.

Surely, a place that saw to the beauty of end-of-season flowers would certainly see to the comfort of end-of-life patients. I brushed my fingers over the mixed vegetation, disrupting a butterfly from its task. It flitted off, its color fading in the distance.

A phone trilled, and I jerked around, scanned the front porch, the drive, and the widespread lawn. Nobody in sight, and the phone still rang. And then it hit me, the phone was mine. No one had my number. No one knew where I was. Keagan's name flashed across my screen, and my heart did a double take. Somebody cared.

"Hello," I said cautiously.

"Hey, Holly." His voice wrapped around me like a warm blanket. "I'm just checking to see how you are." He couldn't have picked a more perfect time to lend me support.

My double-taking heart did a triple take. I wasn't used to anyone but guards checking on me, and though a part of me liked his caring, another part screamed to watch out. This man could definitely break my heart.

"How did you get my number?" My words sounded harsh. Accusatory.

His pause sounded long. Too long. I'm-saying-goodbye long. "Took your phone last night. Programmed in my number." He sounded as contrite as a little kid caught with his hand in the cookie jar.

"I would have given you my number." I sounded as bitchy as a retail worker on Black Friday. "All you had to do was ask."

"I should have." True regret colored his voice, and guilt colored mine. I shouldn't have gotten so out of whack over a phone call, but all this was coming at me pretty fast, and I wasn't sure if I stood on firm ground.

I slumped against the wall. "It's no big deal. Whatcha need?"

"To know how you are." Lightness returned to his voice, and I felt all was forgiven. "How are you, and where are you?" He didn't say one thing and mean another. He said it like he saw it, not always tactful, but I found his approach somewhat charming.

"I'm standing outside Castle Care, terrified to go in." The thought of entering paralyzed me. "What if it's an awful place?" These were the times when being alone sucked.

"I'll stay on the phone. Let's go in together." His voice encouraged me to take the next step. "Are you ready?" His soothing tone coaxed me to move toward the front of the building. "Holly, are you ready?"

I could do this. He would be here with me. I wouldn't be alone.

"Yes." I quickly yanked open the door, like I was ripping off a Band-Aid. Better torn rapidly than peeled slowly. Thankfully, Keagan remained on the line to provide aftercare.

A strangled cry squeaked from my lips.

"What?" Concern filled his voice.

Tears filled my eyes. A whimper snuck past my lips.

"Damn it, Holly, what the hell is happening?"

"It's beautiful." And it was. "Oh, Keagan, there's an indoor pond and a waterfall." I walked the perimeter of the pond and looked at the colorful fish that swam to the edge, opening their mouths as if to greet me. "Everything's amazing."

"Shit, Holly, don't scare me like that. I thought I was going to have to come find you."

I came to an abrupt stop. To think he'd leave what he was doing to comfort me was laughable, but endearing.

"You're too sweet, but if it makes you feel better, the cemetery was sad, and I could use some comforting."

"I'm your man and happy to offer all the comfort you need." There was definitely more to his offer than comfort, and I was looking forward to investigating. "As long as you're okay, I'm gonna run. The new guy needs direction." It was funny how he wouldn't say Cole. Silencing his name didn't make him go away.

Cole held no interest for me. He didn't have the same bipolar swagger that Keagan did, and even though Keagan was all over with his behavior, I liked that he took me to a safe place in the end.

"I'll see you tonight," I whispered before I hung up the phone and walked around the tranquil pond. Within minutes, I was back at the front door where I started.

"May I help you?" The receptionist sat tucked out of the way in a corner. Her desk didn't fight with the peaceful serenity of the running water and swimming koi.

"I'm Holly McGrath, and my mother was here nearly two years ago." If ever a girl appeared sweet and compassionate, this one did. "You probably don't remember her, but I wanted to come by and say thanks for taking care of her. I was hoping I could talk to your director."

A look of recognition crossed her face. "Your mom was Connie, right?"

I was stunned the young girl would remember her name. It had been twenty-one months since my mom passed. Dying people came and went, but rarely were they remembered.

"Your mom talked about you nonstop. She was so proud of you. We all felt like we knew you. Between you and me," she looked around the empty room, "you got a raw deal. That was a total setup."

I lifted my shoulders and sighed. It wasn't the first time I'd been told that, but it was over and done with. "It was a tragedy all the way around."

"Just hang on a minute." She picked up the phone. "Mr. Conley. Connie McGrath's daughter is here."

"Oh, I don't want to bother anyone..." But the words were barely out before a graying, spindly old man shuffled into the foyer. He had a warm smile and the charisma of a seasoned politician.

"So, you're Connie's daughter." He patted my back in a grandfatherly manner, immediately making me comfortable in his presence. "It's a pleasure meeting you, Holly. I'm Stan Conley."

"Sadly, I wasn't able to be with my mom when she passed." The reality of the situation tore me up. "It was important for me to see where her final days were spent." I looked around the entry and smiled. In spite of the less than ideal circumstances, my mom would have been happy here.

"She sure seemed happy here." He led me down a hallway. "She missed you desperately but had good friends around her. Let's take a tour."

We walked down a hallway that contained rooms that were more bedroom than hospital room. They were comforting and homey, with warm colors, soft sheets, and tranquil music. A place where a person could find a peaceful end. At each turn, I held my breath, waiting for the awful to appear.

With each step, the heaviness of my heart lifted. Knowing my mom had been in a caring home with people who had paid attention to her was a soothing balm to my injured soul. She'd had a place where a person could find a peaceful end.

We stopped in front of something Stan called the Wall of Fame. A picture of my mom was posted among hundreds of others. She was sitting in the café, sipping coffee. In front of her was a picture of me. In spite of our distance, she was still enjoying coffee with me.

"Mr. Conley," I touched my mom's face once more before we moved down the hallway, "prior to my incarceration, I was an RN. I'm trying to get my license back, and I'm told volunteering could gain me favor. Could I do that here?"

Working here could offer me an ideal situation. I could get the volunteer component I needed out of the way, and I could be connected to my mom again. At least be connected to the people who saw her last.

"You want to volunteer here?" The man perked up, making himself at least an inch taller.

"Obviously, I can't work in a nursing capacity, but I can read to people or sit with them." I glanced over my shoulder at the picture of my mom. "I'm not sure if my arrest record would hinder my ability to volunteer, but yes, I'd love to volunteer here. I need an opportunity to prove my worth."

He placed his hands on my shoulders. It was the kind of stance a person took when they delivered bad news. "Many of our patients use medicinal marijuana to ease their pain and depression. You got caught in a bad deal, wrong place at the wrong time."

"You say wrong place at the wrong time, but I'm guilty. I did the crime, and I did the time."

"And time can change everything."

"Thanks for your understanding."

That was the irony of it all. I was arrested in October. With the passage of Amendment 64 and the legalization of marijuana fourteen months later, everything would have been different.

"Unfortunately, marijuana is still a federal crime." He guided me back toward the pond. "I don't see the nursing board being all that flexible with you, but if volunteering will help, come as often as you feel necessary. Everyone here has value."

"Thanks, Mr. Conley. You made my day in so many ways." The uncertainty of my mom's last days had finally been resolved. "I can see you run a loving home. I know she spent her final days in a place where she felt at peace." I threw my arms around the old man and hung on. "Thank you." It was clear Mom had been in the second best place she could have been. The first would have been in my arms.

I walked to the porch, feeling fresh and renewed. I tapped out Carla's phone number from memory. I'd used my quota of courage for the day. I was taking the coward's approach by texting. The talking would come soon enough.

Carla,
We need to talk. I'm on my way to the hospital.
Holly

My phone pinged, and my heart jumped.

Sorry, won't be there. Text me next week, and I'll try to put you on my calendar.
Carla - Shift Supervisor

Carla's "I'll put you on the calendar next week" surged my blood. Her "Shift Supervisor" sent me into a rage.

Carla,

How about coffee? We need to talk.
Holly

Within seconds, she responded.

Holly,

Not interested. As far as the letter, I'll think about it, but I need to consider the impact of writing a letter for a convicted drug dealer. I have my job to think about.

Carla

The more I thought about Carla's statement, the angrier I got. It was her boyfriend, my ex who had established the connection. On some level, he was responsible. Sure, I made the call. I asked for the goods, but where in the hell did that dealer come from? After all this time, I'd never thought to ask.

The foot of a giant bitch had crushed my optimism. I sat in the Jeep, shaking and damn near wrenching the steering wheel off the column. Any warmth I'd felt ran cold as I drove the twenty miles to the hospital.

The familiar speeding of my heart began as the rush of adrenaline pumped through me. The unknown of the emergency room was always exciting. Today was no different, except there would be no blood or broken bones.

In spite of feeling scared and insecure, I walked into the hospital with my shoulders back and my head high.

Most of the faces had changed; only a few had remained the same. Some looked down their noses and turned their shoulders. Others responded with a squeal or a hug.

Maggie, the intake coordinator, was a squealer. She bounced up and down enough to count as a cardio workout.

"You're such a sight for my tired eyes. When are you coming back?" Maggie tried to pull me through the secured door, but I resisted. "They put that condescending bitch in your place. She's Attila the Hun in blue scrubs."

I pulled from her grip. I wasn't an employee, and I didn't want to risk her job. I had enough guilt in my life. I wasn't adding Maggie's job loss to it.

"I lost my license, Maggie. I'm only here to ask a few people to write letters on my behalf. Is Dr. Becker around?" Her eyes squinted, and her lips pursed. She was obviously not a fan of the man they called Dr. Hottie.

"I'm aware of his relationship with Carla." I patted her back to reassure her. "You don't need to sidestep that situation."

"Oh Holly, you should have seen the way she carried on when they sentenced you. She wasn't the grieving friend. She was the joyous victor. I'm telling you, she's the reincarnation of Hitler." She pulled me toward the white phone on the wall. "I'll page Dr. Becker for you." She picked up the phone and spoke. Her voice echoed through the hall. *Dr. Becker to the ER...Dr. Becker to the ER.* "By the way, Carla should be here any minute. Her shift begins at three."

I fisted my hands and shoved them in my front pockets. That bitch had lied to me. Hopefully, I could get what I needed and get out quickly. I'd changed my mind about seeing her. There was a real possibility I might hit her if I got close enough.

Matt rounded the corner. He looked like he didn't have a care in the world. "Hey, how are you?" He slid up next to me, as if two years hadn't passed and he wasn't living with Satan.

"Hanging in there."

Maggie walked behind Matt and flipped him off.

I wished I was free to laugh. "I just wanted to remind you to write a letter to the board on my behalf. You know how important this is to me." He closed in and caged me against the wall. I had nowhere to go when he leaned in. "Back off, Dr. Becker; you're too close for comfort."

The asshole gave me an arrogant, cocksure smile. "I used to give you a lot of comfort." He dropped one hand to my cheek and moved it toward my lips. I swore to myself if that man touched my mouth, I'd bite him.

"You gave me a lot of things; comfort wasn't one of them, and thankfully neither was herpes." I stepped to the side. *Shit, what was I doing? This wouldn't get me a letter.* "We've both moved on, Matt." It nearly killed me to smile at him, but I needed something, and I hoped a smile was all it would cost me. "What about Carla?"

"She's a fucking bitch." He swung away from me and leaned on the wall. "She left me in the parking lot and made me call a cab. Since then, she's locked me out of the apartment and her pants. This is *your* fault."

My fault? I reminded myself that this little field trip had one purpose, which was to secure several letters from my peers. "You owe me, Matt. You owe me for all the times you cheated on me. You owe me for hooking up with my friend. Most of all, you owe me because I deserve to have something good in my life, and you have the power to help make that happen."

"Shall we barter?" He leaned in until his body rubbed against mine. His voice was barely above a whisper. "I miss burying myself in you." Keagan was right, Matt wouldn't give me something for nothing. "I'll write the letter, but I want you in return."

With a push on his chest, he was knocked backward a foot or so. "I wonder what would happen if everyone knew you got me that connection? You wouldn't go to jail, and you'd most likely keep your job, but what about upward mobility? A whiff of scandal would definitely keep you from becoming chief."

My words stopped him cold. I had no idea if that were true, but neither did Matt. "Do the right thing and send the damn letter." I had written the address for the board on a slip of paper I tucked in his lab coat. "I expect a stellar review encompassing my skills and professionalism."

When I turned, Carla stood at the end of the hall. The heat in her expression could curdle milk.

"Hey, Carla." I nodded in her direction, but she disappeared behind a secure door.

Maybe I should have followed her and tried to smooth out the wrinkles; instead, I made my rounds and managed to secure two promises from hospital staff. Combined with Matt's, I would have the three I needed. I'd done all I could do. Now it was up to the board.

Next stop was the grocery store, then home. I hoped Keagan had an appetite for more than lasagna. I hoped what I offered would be satisfying.

Chapter 12

KEAGAN

Damn poacher. Holly showed up around four, and the workday all but ended. The new guy couldn't seem to keep his eyes from traveling in her direction. He watched with intensity as she unloaded the groceries from her car and brought them inside her cabin. His eyes went back and forth, back and forth, like a pendulum. He was wasting my fucking time. The dumb ass was so involved in watching her, he got a splinter the size of a log wedged in his hand.

"If you want to live until tomorrow, I suggest you pay attention to what you're doing." It would serve him right if the damn thing got infected.

"It's just a splinter." He picked at the piece of timber. "I've had worse."

"Not referring to the splinter, asshole. My girl's off limits." I'd never been possessive, but holy hell, the new guy devoured her with his eyes. "You look at her again like that, and I promise to break your fucking face."

His head snapped back like I'd landed an uppercut to his chin. "I didn't know she was your girl. At the grocery store, she said it was a first date. Can't a guy admire beauty?"

"No." No one would devour her but me, and I'd better get on that soon. The vultures were lining up to take the first bite. "Finish stalls eighteen through twenty-two, then pull the horses from the field." He wanted to admire beauty. I'd be happy to show him beauty. I'd give him a first class view of a horse's ass. "I'll see you tomorrow morning at five."

I snuck into my cabin to shower and shave before my date. The first day we met had been sketchy, the second held promise, but tonight I'd make her mine.

The aroma of pasta sauce seeped through my bedroom window, and my stomach growled. I was hungry, but pasta wasn't the only thing I craved. I feared my hunger could only be satisfied by her.

Fifteen more minutes.

This is bullshit.

I picked up the cake, grabbed a bottle of wine and headed next door. What did my father say about promptness? *Tardiness robbed us of opportunities.* I couldn't wait another minute to kiss Holly.

She greeted me in a flowered dress, cowboy boots, and a smile. If my damn hands weren't full of wine and cake, I'd have grabbed her and kissed her like I'd wanted to all day.

Her lips touched mine in a disappointing quickie that wouldn't suffice. I rushed to the kitchen to unload my offerings and pulled her into my arms.

"You're gorgeous."

"You're early."

"I couldn't wait."

"You're forgiven."

Somewhere between I would never date a convict and would you have dinner with me, she'd become mine. The only thing left was to convince her she wanted me, too.

My lips lingered on hers, tasting the sweetness she offered. Let's face it, a kiss would never be just a kiss. A kiss said a lot about a person. A quick peck said, "Hi, you're okay." A French kiss showed intense interest. When your lips were attracted to each other like a magnet to metal was when you knew you shared more than raw passion or simple attraction.

Unbreakable connection.

Unbreakable until we both needed air.

"Dinner smells amazing." I knew the taste of the meal would pale in comparison to the taste of her.

When she looked at me, the world was silenced. I swore I could hear her heart beat in rhythm with my own.

Unambiguously congruent.

"I made lasagna and very garlicky bread." She scrunched her nose. "We both have to eat the bread. It's the only way to make it fair."

I nibbled at her lip, and her smile unfolded.

Undeniable conclusion.

She was mine.

We started with the bread. The woman could cook. My burgers paled in comparison to her lasagna. She would make any Italian mama proud. Comfortable at her table, we talked about our day.

Jealousy reared its ugly head when she mentioned seeing Matt at the hospital. I was right about him. I knew he'd want something in return for the letter. It took every bit of self-restraint to remain seated. My fists itched to punch his arrogant face to the back of his skull, to shove his boathouse shoes so far up his ass, he could tie the laces with his teeth.

Instead, I sat and listened and pretended not to be a ball of seething anger. Holly was happy and proud. She'd solved her problem and found her power; I was proud of her and too damn far away. I tugged her into my lap. Her happiness was an infectious disease I was happy to contract.

"See, you don't need people who bring nothing of value to your life. You need happiness and love." I wouldn't tell her yet, but all she needed was me.

"And dessert." She licked my lips, and my balls tightened. Trouble. She was the right kind of trouble.

"I'll give you dessert." I stood with her in my arms and took her straight to bed. Never before had I felt the primal need to claim a woman. She was mine, and in a moment she would be mine completely. Everything would change the moment I sank myself inside her body.

Fear and uncertainty no longer framed her features. My lips claimed her with fevered passion. No words could explain the emotions I felt having her in my arms, so I attempted to show her.

Like a nervous teenager, I pulled her dress over her head. Any onlooker would have thought I was a virgin from the way I fumbled with her bra. My hands shook as I slid her panties down her long legs. I considered removing her boots, but she looked so sexy wearing them and nothing else.

Her beautiful body was sweeter than chocolate cake. Even my voice trembled as I told her she was perfect in every way. Doubt surfaced in her eyes.

"Erase the recording going on in your head. When I say you're beautiful, you are." I may have sounded gruff, but damn it, I didn't want anyone else's words running through her brain.

"Yes, it's just—." I silenced her with a kiss. A perfect kiss.

"No just. You're perfect. You're mine." Her eyes widened for a second, then softened as my declaration set in. Her hand threaded through my hair, and she held on just as tightly as I did.

"This isn't a one-night thing." I wasn't ready to declare undying love, but I envisioned her being in my life in a week, in a year, in ten years. That should have scared the shit out of me, but it didn't. "This is bigger. I don't know why, but it is. If you can't handle that, say so now. I'm not going to offer my heart and have you rip it to shreds." I'd been down that road. Gave my heart to a girl, and she gave her body to another. Not happening this time. Her silence unsettled me. Was she considering not moving forward?

"Don't hate me tomorrow." Her eyes pleaded with me not to hurt her.

I deserved her caution. Since she arrived, I'd acted like a man with a personality disorder.

"I'll never do that to you again."

She worked the buttons of my shirt with shaking fingers. Impatient, I worked on my jeans as she finished up top. Pride swelled in my chest as she scanned my body. Tonight was huge; I was hoping to gain some ground in the breeding category.

"My boots," she said. One foot slid toward the heel of the other.

"Are fucking sexy." My tongue lingered on her quickening pulse. The pace picked up the minute my fingers skimmed her hardened nipples. Her breathing stopped as I gently pinched the pebble.

My lips sought out her other breast. I sucked and tugged. "Oh,...Keagan." I pulled a shallow cry from her lips. The need in her voice made my dick pulse. She reached for me and gripped me tightly, nearly ending the evening prematurely.

Releasing her nipple, I hovered over her, the heat of my tongue tracing down her stomach. Poised between her legs, I sat back and stared. Her beautiful body blushed.

Red cowboy boots pressed against my hips, her knees bent. Her eyes were focused on one thing...me, and I'd never felt so certain of anything.

"Dessert. I want dessert." Anticipation glazed her eyes.

There was no way I could wait any longer to taste her. I pulled her to the edge of the bed and dropped to the floor. I had a feeling this wouldn't be the last time she'd bring me to my knees. I dipped my tongue and knew the gates of heaven had just opened.

Moans filled the air as she filled my mouth with her sweetness. Her taste—her scent—was like catnip, and I was the cat. By the end of the evening, there would be no question about us.

Her bundle of nerves throbbed beneath my tongue while her thighs shook. I couldn't deny her any longer. Pulling her gently into my mouth, I massaged the sensitive flesh with my tongue before I slid a finger into her wetness. With gentle probing and soft suckling, I took her over the edge. "Keagan," she cried, causing every nerve in my body to react. My name had never sounded as beautiful as it did slipping from her lips.

My heart sank when I saw the tears running down her cheeks.

"Holly, are you okay?" I had no idea what went wrong. "God, did I hurt you?" She appeared to be enjoying everything. Did I read her wrong? I pulled her into a sitting position and lifted her naked body into my lap. I was at a loss for words.

Set Aside

"Oh, Keagan, I'm sorry. Everything is perfect." She buried her head into my shoulder and sighed. "What you did to me was...unbelievable. I've never felt so beautiful and treasured in my life. I'm overwhelmed with emotion."

I let out the breath I was holding. In that moment, I knew I was halfway in love with her already.

The *thunk* of her boots on the floor echoed through the room. She shifted and straddled me, her wetness teasing my hardness. "You know, Keagan, if we go through with this, everything will change."

"Everything has already changed." My body begged to be buried in hers, but I took my time, memorizing every curve of her body. I loved the way she responded to my hands, my mouth and my words. I couldn't wait to see how she responded to my...

"Keagan, I need you in me now."

All she had to do was ask, and I had my jeans in hand, the condom out of the pocket.

She pulled the condom from my hand and slipped it gently over my bobbing erection. The feel of her fingers as she rolled the latex up my length was heavenly. Poised above her, I leaned in to take her mouth before I slipped myself into her body.

Her sex gripped mine. My body begged for more. Harder. Deeper. Faster. I kept reminding myself it had been years since she'd had sex. I needed to be gentle, to go slowly.

My body demanded more. Shaking, I redirected that need to her mouth. Our tongues tangled; she purred with contentment. The minute our hips met, I sighed. It was more than I could have imagined. Her soft insides squeezed me so beautifully. Her hips rocked to a rhythm she had chosen for us. Slow and sexy we moved. Her eyes looked at mine, and I saw her vulnerability—her doubt.

"It's perfect; you're perfect. You're perfect for me."

If a heart could explode, mine did. I pressed my thumb against her bundle and rubbed in soft circles. I prayed for the restraint I'd need to get her there before I came undone. Her pleasure was important to me. This night was important; it set the standard for the nights to come.

The tenseness started in her hips and extended through her legs. I increased the pressure and pace, knowing I was going to blow any second. Her body stiffened, then shuddered. The sounds she made threw me over the edge. Yes, everything had changed.

Chapter 13

HOLLY

A hint of sunshine peeked through the curtains, straight into my eyes. When I rolled to my side, only cold, crisp sheets embraced me. No body warmth. No strong arms to crawl into. Keagan's side was empty. A divot in the pillow was the only evidence I hadn't slept alone. That and the strain of my deliciously sore muscles.

A glance at the clock, and I knew he'd been up for hours, working the ranch. I rolled out of bed, slid into my robe and walked to my kitchen. I still felt giddy when I pressed the power button on the coffee maker. Such a benign act, and yet so freeing.

The remnants of our half-eaten cake littered the dining room table. I'd spoon fed him the decadent dessert while he'd caressed every inch of me. Who said I couldn't have my cake and eat it, too?

I danced around the table, listening to a song that only played in my head. *Then He Kissed Me* was a song my mother belted out often, and it gave me the perfect beat to clean our mess. With a swish of my hand, I scooped the cake crumbs into the trash bin and went about planning my day.

"Hit the ground running" was my new mantra. Today, I'd be

hitting Mickey up for some riding lessons so I could hold my own in the saddle. Although riding with Keagan had its benefits, he was right: I lived on a ranch, and I'd better get accustomed to ranch life.

An unexpected visit was the perfect time to return her big gift. I didn't need something so grand in my life. Sometimes bigger wasn't better.

I was happy with how things were turning out. I had a home, friends, and a man who made me feel like I was spun from gold.

Once showered and dressed, I stepped onto the creaking porch and let the morning sun warm my face. It was the simple pleasures that made life worthwhile. The heat of the sun. The smell of a flower. And the feel of a virile man between my legs.

Voices carried in the breeze, and I scanned the field, settling on the crowd in front of the barn. Mickey would live a thousand deaths before she was forgiven for leaving a vibrator hung like a donkey in my drawer, and I would never embarrass her in front of a client, but her staff was a different matter.

I marched over to the barn, where Mickey was talking to Cole and the McKinleys. In one hand was an unopened package of D batteries, in the other a piece of rubber that drew the attention of every cowboy in the barn. I wasn't discreet; I'd brandished it like a weapon when I marched in full view of the men.

"Can you believe what this woman put in my drawer?"

I wielded the rubber penis like a sword and swung it toward every man present. I'd never seen men stagger back so fast. A passerby might have thought I'd whipped out a loaded gun.

"Holly, put that damn thing away." Cole swatted at the jumbo dildo when I came for him.

I had to admit, I took great pleasure in their discomfort. It was nice to know a ten-inch piece of silicone could shut them up. "I won't be needing this, Mickey." I tossed the vibrator into the air and watched it flip end over end until it came to rest at the tip of Mickey's boot. The men jolted back farther, like I'd tossed napalm at their feet. "My needs are being met."

Keagan stepped forward, puffed out his chest, and proudly

declared, "Yes, they are." Public declarations were becoming a thing for us. "Your place or mine tonight?"

"Yours." I placed a rough kiss against his mouth and walked away from the barn. Over my shoulder, I called to Mickey, "Coffee. My place. When you're finished." Her cheeks were as red as freshly picked cherries.

I'd barely made it into my cabin before Mickey ran up the steps behind me. Her hands were suspiciously empty.

"Where's your toy?" I teased.

"I made Cole take it to the main house." Her shoulders shook as she laughed. "You would have thought I'd handed him a poisonous snake."

"To a man, that massive thing is worse than a snake. Just looking at it can devour a man's ego. At least Keagan was a good sport about it. Hell, the thing barely fit in my drawer...how was I supposed to fit it...?" I shuddered at the thought.

"Megan comes home next. We'll hide it in her drawer. We'll make it the official post-prison mascot." Her smile was Hitchcock perfect.

I felt young and carefree, chatting with a friend in my home. I wasn't worried about getting my license back; I was plotting to damage the impressionable mind of a young ex-con.

Megan was twenty-five but quiet and reserved. She spent most of her days hiding in her bunk. "I'm not sure Megan can handle the sight of that thing."

"Megan can handle more than most people think, but enough about Megan, tell me about Keagan. Was it good?" She walked straight to the cupboard, pulled out two cups, poured the morning's leftover coffee, doctored it up, then came to sit in the living room.

"Oh, Mickey. It was...it was amazing. We need more brothers here for the rest of the girls. I think we're one short." I cradled the coffee mug in my hands and closed my eyes. Behind my lids were visions of Keagan's naked body pressed into mine. Pure bliss.

"There are only four brothers, but maybe one of the girls will swing the other way. The McKinleys have a sister."

She plopped her boots up on my coffee table. The hay that had been stuck in the cuff of her jeans fell to my floor. The life of a rancher. Hay and horse shit.

I played matchmaker for a minute. "Megan's too soft for Killian, and she'd never be with a girl. Natalie, on the other hand, could give Killian a run for his money, but is it smart to mix fire with gasoline?" That's not something I'd want to see.

"We also have Roland. He's an honorary McKinley, and he's nice enough to change Megan's mind about staying single for the rest of her life." We both chewed on that thought for several minutes. Girl time—a guilty pleasure.

Mickey and I chatted for hours. She agreed to teach me to ride, and I agreed to be the on-call nurse at the ranch. It was sweet of her to acknowledge my need to contribute.

After coffee and conversation, I walked her out. She stood on the porch, looking at my collection of pumpkins, and wholeheartedly agreed that a carving contest was in order. With Halloween around the corner, we agreed the weekend would be perfect. She dashed off to do ranch stuff while I ran to the bathroom to prepare for tonight's date. How easy it was to get addicted to Keagan.

FOR THE NEXT FEW DAYS, my mornings were spent volunteering at the center, and my nights were spent in the arms of Keagan. I'm not sure whose appetite was larger, his or mine. All I knew was I would never get enough of him. We had a soul connection, and I felt hollow when we weren't together.

In many ways we were alike, and in many we weren't. He struggled with his birth position. I struggled with my birth. We both struggled with the need to be validated. We both needed somewhere to belong. We both used work as a gauge of self-worth.

I'd been passed up and passed on enough to know attention was fleeting and love was fickle. After the experience with Matt, I realized my problem was me. I expected very little from others, and people rarely disappointed.

Set Aside

Today, the ranch was bustling with bodies. Materials were being delivered for the barn upgrades, and Keagan was working with Cole to get him accustomed to how things were done at M and M. He wasn't thrilled with the ranch hand, but I imagined it had nothing to do with his work ethic or his ability. Cole was overly friendly, and Keagan was jealous.

He'd have to come to terms with other men being around me. We lived on a ranch, and men were constantly coming and going. For now, I'd deal with it.

Mickey had decided to let the 4-H club hold a mini rodeo in her arena in the spring, which meant she was buried in paperwork, but she made time for a daily riding lesson.

I'd been spending my days at Castle Care getting to know the patients. The thought of final wishes never left my mind. Sadly, many people were no longer coherent, but I read them stories and held their hands. I wiped sweat off brows and drool off lips. Dignity was important when you were helpless.

The families were generous with their time and were happy to reminisce about their loved ones with me. Most were touched I cared to ask, and when I explained my situation, they understood my need to help others. I couldn't be there for my parent, but I could be there for theirs.

Mrs. Lakewood was still spry and attentive when she wasn't in excruciating pain. Pancreatic cancer was brutal. When her pain was tolerable, she taught me how to play hearts and kicked my butt every time she pulled out the cards. She told me about her travels and how she loved Paris in the spring.

"What did you love most about Paris?" I asked.

She sat quietly, reflecting. I expected her answer to be the Louvre or the Arc De Triumph. Hell, I would have even expected poodles and French berets.

Her weakened voice trembled. "I loved having strong coffee and croissants from a sidewalk cafe. The world could be happening around me, but I'd get lost in the moment." She sat on her bed looking dreamy while her memories played the reel from that time in her life.

Her answer was so simple. Could the joys of life be found in a croissant? What about a man? A kiss?

Since she would never have the opportunity to travel to Paris again, I would bring Paris to Mrs. Lakewood. I arranged to have cafe tables set up near the pond. French music played from a boombox hidden in the corner. I baked croissants and brought fresh jam and real butter.

Mr. Conley had a picture of the Eiffel Tower blown up and placed on the wall behind the cafe tables. It appeared we were looking at the landmark through the window of a cafe. Her family was invited to join us for breakfast.

When Mrs. Lakewood was wheeled into the area, she cried. I served her family coffee and pastries while donning a red beret. She reminisced with her family about their lives together. I did my best to stay out of the way and let them have family time. I wished I'd been allowed a final cup of coffee with my mother.

I had so many questions I would have liked to ask her. Things like: who was her first kiss? What did it feel like for her to fall in love? Why did she like to eat jalapeños with her popcorn? Why did she put honey in her coffee? Those were the silly questions I thought about after she was gone.

It's not the big moments you miss; those, you remember well. It's the smaller moments you didn't take the time to savor. The way she braided my hair or the way she massaged my shoulders from the outside in.

I snapped pictures from my hiding place in the corner. They would be developed today and put in an album tonight. Mrs. Lakewood didn't have much time. It was like that with pancreatic cancer. Here today—gone tomorrow.

Today would be added to the long list of memories her family could keep. Her life would be remembered for her kind spirit, her loving disposition, and her wicked card skills.

It didn't take much to make a person feel valued. It was easy to smile at someone or ask about their day. Yes, the simple things had value.

Set Aside

Why did the world spend so much time focused on the incidentals when the important stuff was waiting for their attention?

When Mrs. Lakewood's field trip to Paris was finished, I cleaned the lobby and went to visit Mr. Hadaway. He had congestive heart failure and was a ticking time bomb. His blood pressure couldn't be controlled, and the swelling of his extremities made it difficult for him to get around. He had good days and bad. Today was a good day. He asked me to read the Farmer's Almanac to him. We only had last year's volume. He laughed at weather predictions and guffawed over the article about daylight savings time.

"Who in the hell decided we could save time? If that were possible, I would have canned a bunch up so I could use it now when I need it."

"Daylight savings time was designed so we could make better use of the daylight hours. It was supposed to reduce energy use."

"That's just hogwash," he grumbled.

"You realize the idea of daylight savings time has been around since Ben Franklin."

"See, just goes to show you what a bunch of rubbish it is. He's the same guy who flew a kite in the rain. What an idiot."

I didn't point out that Ben Franklin invented the lightning rod, the Franklin stove, and the odometer, not to mention the fact that he'd signed *The Declaration of Independence*. If Mr. Hadaway wanted to think Ben Franklin was an idiot, who was I to argue?

We moved our conversation from Ben Franklin to Mr. Hadaway. He spent his youth branding cattle. After finding out I lived on M and M ranch, our conversation turned to livestock and horses. I didn't know anything about either, but I imagined by the end of his life, he would make sure I knew the difference between a mare and a gelding and which end the food went in and which end the food came out. He didn't give me much credit.

He thought it was funny my boyfriend was a cowboy, and the only thing I knew about horses was the difference between a tail and a mane. *Was Keagan my boyfriend?* We hadn't really defined our relationship. I just knew it was more than sex.

After visiting Mr. Hadaway, I went to see Jasper Felding. He was in the final stages of Alzheimer's. No one came to visit him; I wasn't sure if it was because he had no one or because it was heartbreaking for them to come and not be recognized. Alzheimer's is a thief. It steals memories and time. The hardest hit are the ones left behind. How did they cope, knowing their mother or father had no idea who they were?

Jasper sat in bed and stared into space. The lights were on, but his apartment was vacant. I was convinced he could still hear me, so I sang to him. I carried a tune like a blind man with a spear. I stabbed at it but rarely hit my mark.

It didn't matter to Jasper; he didn't complain, and he never asked me to shut up. Eyes forward, he stared at the wall while I belted out my rendition of Amazing Grace.

"Holly, I need to see you in my office." Mr. Conley gave me a weak smile and walked down the empty hallway.

"Okay," I said and followed close behind. I hoped he wasn't unhappy with me. Many times, I imagined I'd overstepped my boundaries, but I felt like a dying person should have what they wanted, whether it was a Rueben on rye or their fingernails painted the perfect red.

I was a pleaser, and doing those things gave my pleaser instinct someplace to reside.

His office was hidden in the corner of the facility. It wasn't beautifully appointed with nice furniture or expensive art. He worked from a conference table that sat in the center a beige room. No wonder my mom liked him; he was a humble man who spent his money with care and consideration for his patients.

"Come in, come in." He flagged me in and let the door shut behind us.

We weren't alone; a woman sat at the table. She reminded me of a young Julie Andrews from *The Sound of Music*. I waited for her to begin belting out "Edelweiss", but she didn't. She sat in front of her lined yellow notepad and waited.

"Holly, this is Joyce Cumberland. She runs an organization called Finishing Touches."

The women offered me her hand.

Set Aside

"It's a pleasure to meet you, Ms. Cumberland."

I grasped her hand firmly and gave it a shake. My mother always told me to refer to people by 'Miss' if I wasn't sure of their marital status. Nowadays, many people wore rings on both hands or none. What used to be a simple giveaway was no more.

"May I call you Holly?" She pushed her pen to the top of the pad and leaned back in her chair.

"Absolutely." I had no idea why she was there. Finishing Touches sounded like an interior design firm. Maybe Stan was going to do something with his simple office space. How I figured into the mix was a mystery to me. "Have you heard of Make a Wish Foundation, Genie in a Bottle, or Dream Foundation?"

"I'm familiar with two of the three you mentioned. They're wish fulfillment organizations for the terminally ill."

My interest was piqued. I'd been thinking about wish fulfillment for a while. Whether it was my wish to get my license or Mrs. Lakewood's desire to eat pastries in Paris, wishes were harbingers of hope, and no one should be left without hope.

"Right."

Stan took a seat next to Joyce and offered me the one across from her. "Joyce is a friend of mine. I was talking to her about your volunteer hours and how connected you are to our patients. She wanted to meet you and talk to you about an opportunity."

Did my volunteer work open other opportunities? I wasn't looking for anything but redemption when I began volunteering here. If I couldn't pay Mr. Conley and his staff for their kindness to my mom, then I would pay it forward.

Working at Castle Care Center had given me a place to go while the world continued to spin. My professional life was stalled, waiting for the board to decide my fate.

"Let's start at the beginning," Joyce said. I swear, the lyrics to "Do-Re-Mi" began to play in my head. "We are a wish fulfillment organization. We are nonprofit. We work with an older population. Our budget isn't as large as some, but we do have generous benefactors. Stan tells me you've been doing a bit of wish granting yourself."

At first I wasn't sure if I'd been interfering with her work, but her smile told me she was pleased I cared enough to do something. "Oh,...well,...yes. Although, I wouldn't say what I do is on par with anything a large organization could do. I do what I can. I'm limited by what I have left in my checking account, and what I can rummage up around the center." To say my resources were stretched was a vast understatement.

"This could be your lucky day. I can't offer you full-time yet. However, I have a half-time position available." She grabbed her pen and doodled on her yellow pad. A sunshine. I liked her outlook. "You would be working with me to figure out what our clients want in order to put the finishing touches on their lives."

Ah...now I got the name. Clever. "Wow, that's amazing. You do understand I'm trying to get my nursing license back, right?" I fidgeted in my chair. Any talk of my license had me squirming. "Has Stan given you all the facts surrounding me? I have a felony conviction for drugs. I just got out of prison." Full disclosure was important. Hadn't there been enough secrets and sneakiness in my life? New life. New expectations.

"I'm aware of the obstacles you face. I've been friends with Stan for years." She looked at the man sitting next to her. Her eyes warmed with something that told me they were more than friends.

"I just want to make sure you have the whole story. Honesty is important to me, so is loyalty. I owe it to myself to do everything I can to regain my license, but in the interim I would love to help you out. Can we agree on a trial basis? I can't commit to anything long-term at this point."

"I appreciate your honesty. It's a rare quality in this day and age. A trial basis seems prudent." Tucked into the top crease of her yellow pad was a business card. She slipped it out of the crease and into my hand. "Meet me here Monday at eight, and we'll go over the details."

Stunned, I stood still while they slipped out of the door. *Did I just say yes to a job? Did I want the job?* I needed a job for now, and it was a perfect opportunity, but it was the right now job, not necessarily the right job.

With a smile on my face, I headed home to tell Keagan the news.

When I pulled in front of my cabin, a dusty BMW was parked in my spot. On my front porch, wearing rolled up jeans, dock shoes, and a salacious smile was Matt. He sure did know how to turn a good day into disaster.

Chapter 14

HOLLY

"Hey Hols, long time no see, baby. How are you?" He rocked forward to stand, but I threw up my hand, halting his progress.

"What are you doing here, Matt?" He sat in the porch rocker, looking so out of place. His outfit screamed for a boat and a rowing crew. The fact that we were in a landlocked state made it funny. My former attraction to him was a mystery. "You weren't invited."

"I came to see you. Is it so odd I'd care about how you're doing?" He raised his eyes in a way that once made me swoon. Now it left me with a bellyache.

My preference leaned toward rugged men dressed in jeans and cowboy boots. I wanted the smell of the outdoors to hug me, calloused hands to caress me. I'd take cow manure over hand sanitizer any day.

That thought rocked me. *Wasn't I the one desperate to get back into the hospital?* Yes, but it didn't mean I was desperate for the trappings. It was the job I wanted, not the people. *Shouldn't it be about the people?* Yes. The right people? The patients?

"Why are you here?" There was no misconstruing my tone. I

Set Aside

didn't want him here. This was my happy place, and he was mucking it up with his presence.

"I sent your letter and tried to convince Carla to do the same." His nose turned up the way mine used to when raw sewage had flooded the prison showers. "She's a hard sell, but as you know, I can be quite persuasive." God, the man was arrogant.

"Thanks for taking one for the team." It was a shitty thing to say, but Carla and Matt were made from the same cloth. Broadcloth, and they were both trying to convince the world they were silk. My cowboy had a higher thread count than the two of them together. I hadn't been a ranch-loving girl, but I'd turned into a rancher-loving girl.

"I aim to please." His voice carried a cocky swagger.

"You didn't need to deliver the news in person."

"There's a little issue about a threat. Are we square now?"

I couldn't believe he thought I'd follow through with my threat. "Yep, we're square. You can go now."

He leaned toward me. "Tell me, when will you be finished slumming?" I backed away and plopped myself on the steps across from him.

"When will you?" I wasn't referring to Carla, I was referring to every woman who slipped into the mop closet with that asshole, including me.

"So you admit to slumming. I get it. The world is a buffet." He licked his lips while staring at mine. "Why not nibble here and there? There's no sense in eating off the same plate when there's such a variety to choose from. Who wants to taste the same flavor every day?"

Piece by piece, he visually plucked the clothes from my body. I shivered as if I sat bare and the wind had whipped across my skin.

"I like eating from the same plate each day. There's comfort in knowing what you're going to get. I've tried fish, and I've tried steak. I prefer steak."

"I'm steak." His arrogant voice rang out.

"You're not steak, that's for sure." Keagan was steak. He was an incredibly tender filet. He was a flavorful porterhouse. He was a lean New York strip.

"You're saying I'm fish. You're cruel." He leaned forward, closing the distance I'd placed between us. "There was a time I was your steak."

"The only steak you were interested in being was tube steak. I deserved more than that."

"What the hell happened to you in prison? Tube steak? I would have never imagined you'd say anything like that. You're making me laugh."

"Glad I can entertain you." Rising from my seated position, I stood at the edge of the porch. He needed to leave. I had good news to share with my friends, and Matt was wasting my precious time. "I have stuff to do, Matt. Thanks for sending the letter."

In three steps, I was at my door, but it took Matt two to catch me. He pinned me against the beveled wood panel, my cheek pressed uncomfortably against the peephole as I struggled to free myself.

His hands ran down my sides. "I'm sure you can figure out a better way to thank me, Holly." He grabbed my hips and pulled me to his front.

Rage filled me. He had no right. "Stop it," I yelled. Pressing my hips back, I attempted to knock him off balance. He loosened his grip, and I spun around to face him.

"That's better, I prefer this position anyway." He leaned in and tried to kiss me. I turned my head and thwarted his advance. My stomach roiled with revulsion.

"Stop it," I yelled again, only this time I channeled that anger and pushed him with both hands, sending him stumbling down the steps.

"Damn it, Holly. Stop fucking around. It's time to come home. I can have Carla gone in a day."

Keagan appeared, and everything from that point happened in slow motion. His windup was swift and efficient. *Whack*, the crack of flesh against bone echoed through the air. A fountain of blood spurted from Matt's nose.

He didn't have a chance against someone like Keagan. Keagan was all brawn. Matt's muscle was contained in his underdeveloped brain.

I flew off the porch and shoved myself between the two men. Keagan came to a dead stop. The look on his face was as cold and dark as a midwinter storm.

"You're going to step in to protect him?" Keagan stretched his hands and rubbed at his bloody knuckles. "What the hell, Holly?"

I wasn't really defending Matt. I was protecting Keagan from a lawsuit. The first punch was warranted; the second would have been overkill.

"You don't have to hit him again. He felt it the first time." I ran into my house and grabbed a roll of toilet paper. Pushing it into Matt's bloody hands, I directed him toward his car. Keagan stood as rigid as a corpse. His lifeless eyes stabbed at my heart. *What the hell was I supposed to do?* Let them fight it out like pugilists?

Just before entering his car, Matt yelled, "When you're done slumming, you know where to find me." Looking past me, his next message was for Keagan. "You'll be hearing from my lawyer."

Keagan grumbled something, but I didn't look his way. I wanted to make sure Matt left. The ranch didn't need that kind of drama. I didn't contribute anything of value, and I certainly wasn't going to contribute anything negative.

When I turned around, Keagan was gone. I ran toward the stables and the sound of horses. Keagan's horses talked to him, and they sounded unhappy.

He needed to understand I didn't need him to defend me. Two years ago, maybe, but not now. I had to learn how to navigate my world. I had to be the designated driver.

When I reached the stables, he was gone. A cloud of dust kicked up in his wake. He was definitely pissed off. His anger seemed to be directed at me. Matt was the one bleeding, but Keagan looked to be the wounded one. He had glowered at me like I'd broken some kind of rule.

I sat in the porch swing for hours. The wind began to whistle between the buildings, and my shivering got the best of me. Finally,

I decided to go in when the grumble in my stomach became louder than the whistling of the cold wind rushing off the prairie.

About a half hour later, I heard the whinny of the horses and knew he'd returned. I wasn't sure if I should go to him or let him come to me. In the end, I opted to give him space. He obviously needed it; otherwise, he wouldn't have taken off.

The rest of the night, I kept one ear tuned to the house next door. His music was loud. Country ballads about broken hearts and cheating girlfriends filled the air.

Did he think I was cheating? We hadn't spent a night apart since our first night together. He couldn't actually believe I'd go back with Matt, could he?

I gnawed on the possibility. The more I thought about it, the angrier I got. I was many things, but I wasn't a cheater. I'd never stoop low enough to betray the person I loved. Infidelity did horrible things to self-worth. I'd never do that to another person.

By the third time the achy breaky heart song played, I was at the end of my tether. It didn't take me long to yank on my shoes and storm across the walkway.

Bang.

Bang.

Bang.

I pounded on the door, trying to get his attention.

Thump.

Thump.

Thump.

My hand slapped against the door. The beat of the music vibrated under my palm.

"Damn it, Keagan," I yelled as the song came to an end. "Open the damn door."

He pulled the door open just as my last word was starting to fade. "What's up?" He rushed to the stereo and turned the volume off.

"What's up? You're asking me what's up?" Oh, I was angrier than I thought I could be. "You punched Matt in the face, then you took off. What the hell is up with you?" Standing on his doorstep, my body shook as my temper flared. He didn't get to stand in front of me and pretend nothing had happened.

"Nothing's up." He raised the longneck bottle in a salute and took a long draw. "I'm listening to music and having a beer."

"What? All of a sudden we don't hang out and eat dinner together? You finish your day and ignore me? Is that how it is with you?"

"You made your choice. You turned around and defended that idiot when I was defending you." There was hurt in his voice. "I hadn't been aware you were slumming when you were with me."

"Oh, grow up. I wasn't defending him. I was trying to get him to leave before you beat him into an unrecognizable heap."

One step back, he distanced himself. "From my standpoint, it didn't look that way. You jumped in between us and begged me to stop. Then you ran inside to get stuff to nurse the cocky bastard."

A growl came from somewhere deep within me. "Your vision is skewed. You saw me shove him off the porch. I wanted him to leave." My voice rose an octave from the beginning to the end of the sentence. "You were right all along. He wanted something for writing the letter. I wasn't offering any payment."

"Why did you step in-between us, Holly?"

"I told you," I screamed, "I didn't want to have to visit you in jail."

We stood in silence and stared at each other. I hated the silence; it was a barrier that kept us apart.

"He's not going to press charges. He's not that stupid. He'll go home and nurse his bloody nose and let Carla nurse his wounded ego. I don't like him around you."

"I don't like him around me either, but that doesn't justify violence. There's no reason to ever respond with your fists. I'd never hit anyone in anger."

"I did, and I'd do it again." His voice echoed through the quiet room. "You might if pushed hard enough."

I couldn't imagine anything getting me spun up enough to hit someone. "You don't have to defend me. I can handle Matt." I stepped into his personal space and put my hand against his cheek.

"I defend what's mine."

"I'm yours Keagan." In my heart I meant it. He was everything I could ever want. "I belong to no other." He was a hardworking man with character. He was loyal, kind, and caring. The one fault I could see was jealousy. We'd have to work on that together.

"Then don't get angry when I defend you. And next time, don't step in the middle. He deserved more than what he got." He covered my mouth with a much-needed kiss. He walked me to the sofa and pulled me into his lap. I heard the clink of glass and the splash of liquid and knew he'd lost his bottle of beer. It didn't matter; that little mistake could be cleaned up later. The mistake I'd made with Keagan needed to be cleaned up now.

I didn't take into consideration he would have felt threatened. If he only knew how I felt about him, he'd have never considered I'd choose any side but his.

Breathless, I pulled back from his lips. In a soft, nurturing voice I said, "You don't need to fight for your place in my heart. You're number one." Sitting on his lap, I peppered his face with kisses. I was hurt he'd doubted my loyalties, but I understood how it felt to not be chosen, and I never wanted him to feel that way again.

"No more fighting. Didn't your mother ever tell you to use your words?"

"No, I grew up on a ranch. You duked it out. The last one standing won." He puffed his chest out with pride. I imagine he was left standing more often than not. Keagan was the type of man to beat life into submission.

"I say we change your mantra to 'make love, not war'."

"I concur" He folded me in his arms and carried me to his bed, where we made good on our new mantra.

Chapter 15

KEAGAN

I loved the peacefulness she found in sleep. Did she dream? And if so, what were those dreams?

Her naked body scooted closer to mine, seeking the heat I offered. It was a sacrifice to stop looking at her, but I wanted to give her the warmth she needed, so I turned her over and pulled her to my chest. She wiggled her bottom into me and sighed.

This was perfect. And to think I almost screwed it up because I was jealous. That asshole touched her, and I'd lost my mind. He had no right putting his hands on my girl.

When Kerrick had told me he'd fallen for Mickey instantly, I'd laughed. That shit didn't happen except in Hallmark movies. That was what I thought until I set eyes on Holly. She flowed through my veins, and I needed her like I needed my type B positive. You couldn't live without blood, and I couldn't live without her. She was all wrong for my lifestyle and all right for my life.

"What are you thinking about?" Her voice was just a whisper, its morning tone soft and sultry.

"You." I pulled her toward me and pressed my lips into her tangled mass of hair. "I was thinking about you." God, she was beautiful.

"Shouldn't you be out with the horses?" She turned around and pressed her lips to my chest. Oh, the tingle raced to my toes.

I ran my hand down her hip. "You want me out with the horses?" Small bumps rose on her skin that had nothing to do with the cold. She responded so readily to my touch.

"No, I want you here with me, but the ranch should be your first priority."

"Priorities change. I'll never shirk my responsibilities to the ranch, and I won't ignore my responsibilities to you either. Right now, I have a responsibility to satisfy you." I buried my face in her neck and nuzzled the soft skin between her ear and shoulder. She was giggling in no time. One of my favorite things was to make her laugh.

We didn't come up for air until lunchtime. I was glad Cole was part of the team and could take on the morning chores. I hated the way he looked at Holly, but he was a good hand, and his presence allowed me to stay in bed.

While she showered, I made bacon, eggs, and toast. Neither of us had eaten last night, and I was starved.

When she came out of the bathroom dressed in one of my flannel shirts and a skimpy pair of panties, the breakfast I made seemed less appetizing, the need to fill my stomach less imminent. However, her growly stomach dictated food was next on the agenda.

She slid into the chair next to me and began to devour her meal. She ate as if she hadn't been fed in days. When she bit into the crisp bacon, she hummed with pleasure. She dipped her toast in the yoke and swiped her plate clean with the end of the crust.

"Tonight is the pumpkin carving contest, and I plan to kick your behind," she said with unmistakable playfulness in her voice. "Mickey and I talked about a fair way to judge, and we decided to let the patients and staff at Castle Care vote. I'll cart the pumpkins over there, provided Mr. Conley is open to the idea."

"That sounds like a good way to do it. I'm sure the staff will get a kick out of what a bunch of ranchers can do to torture a few pumpkins."

"I'm winning. I've got my pumpkin all plotted out in my mind."

Set Aside

"How hard can it be? A couple of triangles here and there and a smiley face, and you're set." I virtually carved a pumpkin in the air, proving I was up to the task.

"You'll lose if you plan on taking the simple route."

"Darlin', I never lose." I gave her an assured look and took a bite of bacon. I was definitely going to lose this contest, but I was going to have fun making her sweat it out.

"Whatever..." She rubbed my leg with her bare foot. She was trying to distract me, and it was working.

I grabbed her cold foot and rubbed it between my warm palms. Her toes curled when I ran my nail up the sole. She let her head fall to the side and sighed.

"Mmm, that sound makes me hungry."

"You just ate." Her voice sounded incredulous.

"I'm hungry for you." I poured on the cowboy twang.

"Oh."

We headed back to bed for another hour. By the time we showered and dressed, the sun was high in the sky.

Holly wanted my help to set up the tables for the carving contest. In exchange, she'd take a ride with me. She'd been training with Mickey, and her seat was solid. As a permanent fixture in my life, she'd need to be able to handle a horse.

Once saddled, I helped her mount Diesel. He would be a good horse for Holly to gain confidence on. Killian had trained him, and he wasn't as spirited as Brody. She settled into the saddle and took charge of the horse with ease.

She was so much more than I'd given her credit for. She had a backbone, and she lived by a set of rules I believed in. Family first, then friends, job, and so on. How I could have questioned her loyalty was beyond me. I could only hope to earn her loyalty and love someday.

"I forgot to tell you. I got a job yesterday at a place called Finishing Touches." She smiled a happy smile, the kind a kid puts on their face when they got their favorite ice cream. "It's a wish fulfillment organization for the terminally ill."

"That's fabulous." She proceeded to tell me about Stan and

Joyce and how they conspired together. "I'm glad you have a plan B."

She stopped Diesel and grimaced. "It's not plan B. It's just until plan A goes through." She pulled the reins so Diesel didn't gobble up the grass beneath his hooves. "Why is everyone so convinced I won't get my license back? I was an excellent nurse with amazing references. That has to account for something."

"We both know they'd be idiots not to reinstate you, but in the event it doesn't go in the direction you were planning, it's good to know there are people who value what you bring to the table." God, I hoped I cleared that up. The last thing I wanted was for her to think I didn't believe in her. I believed in her just fine; it was the system I was unsure about.

"I'm sorry to snap at you. I'm a bit edgy about the whole situation. The letters have been sent, which means the only thing left to do is deliberate. My future lies in their hands." She let her shoulders roll forward.

"You're wrong." My voice was stronger than I meant it to be. Her head bolted up to look at me. "You're in charge of your future. They're only in charge of your nursing license. Being a nurse is the smallest thing about you. You are so much more than that."

She contemplated my statement for a minute. With a nod, she shook the reins and began to trot forward. I pulled up beside her, and we rode in silence to the top of the hill. Once at the top, we dismounted and sat at the edge of the rocky outcropping.

"Where do you see your life going?" she asked. The question caught me off guard. It's one I'd asked myself a lot lately, and the answers kept changing.

"A month ago I'd have said I wanted M and M Ranch to be the best in the world. I would have said I wanted to be viewed as the best breeder in the world." I wrapped my arm around her shoulder and pulled her close to me. She smelled like fresh air and flowers. "I still want those things, but they aren't as important as I once thought."

"What's changed?" She picked at the pebbles beside her and

tossed them off the edge. A clickety-click-clack could be heard as the tiny rocks made their way down the hill.

"You changed everything. Holly, I'm falling in love with you. I never thought it was possible." I felt her body stiffen. Was it too soon to declare? Hell, I didn't know. I'd never been in love before.

She leaned her head into me and said, "I love you, too."

I knew right then this would be one of the best days of my life. We sat on the hilltop under the blue skies, watching the birds fly by. We didn't need to talk; nothing needed to be said. We just existed, and that was enough for now.

WHO WOULD HAVE THOUGHT a bunch of pumpkins could bring out the best and worst in people? We gathered in the arena with our pumpkins and knives. There was plenty of beer and brats, courtesy of Kerrick and Mickey. Alcohol and knives were never a good combination.

Feeling all romantic after a day of lovemaking and sweet words, I sat in the corner and carved a heart in my pumpkin. Next to the heart, I carved out the words Holly, I Choose You. I knew I would take a lot of shit from the guys, but I didn't care. Holly needed to be chosen, and I was the man who'd do it.

About halfway through the event, Cole managed to stab himself. Of course, my little nurse went running to his aid. It was funny to watch Cole pull his hand back and look at me first. When I nodded, he relaxed. I didn't want her touching him, but I wouldn't let the guy bleed to death either.

Mickey ran for the first-aid kit while Holly applied direct pressure. I glanced over his shoulder and shuddered. It probably needed stitches, but Cole would never seek proper medical care. The splinter he got a while back swelled and festered until he lanced it himself. He was a true cowboy, one tough motherfucker.

Holly cleaned and bandaged his wound. He would survive, but the wound would be sore for a few days. She offered to change his bandage daily. Again, he looked at me for permission.

"Stop," she said as she glowered at me.

"What?" I raised my hands in mock surprise.

"You know what. We've talked about the jealous stuff." She dropped Cole's hand and came to climb in my lap. "I belong to you."

"Yes, you do, and he knows it, so...there's no problem." I captured her mouth with mine and felt her melt into me.

Since I had completed my pumpkin, I became Cole's pinch hitter since he couldn't carve his with one hand. We would unveil our creations once everyone was finished.

How he cut himself was a mystery. The man was making a standard jack-o'-lantern. Three triangles and a jagged mouth. He managed to cut more flesh than pumpkin.

Cole and I leaned back and watched the others attack their pumpkins with fervor. Killian, Kerrick, Mickey, and Holly focused on their pumpkins the way I imagined Picasso did his paintings. By the time they were finished, six pumpkins sat with their backs to us. There was nothing like getting shunned by a group of pumpkins.

Holly pulled six flickering battery operated candles from a bag and set one in each pumpkin.

We took turns showing off our creations. There was no prize; it was simply for bragging rights. Holly turned hers around and everyone gasped. She had carved a galloping horse into the outer flesh and left the white pith to glow from behind. It was a work of art, and there was no way she wouldn't win the competition.

When Killian turned his pumpkin around, we all began to laugh. He had carved a whip and a set of handcuffs. There was no way we were going to let the patients at Castle Care see that pumpkin. It was so Killian. How the boy got so twisted, I'd never understand.

"That reminds me," Holly blurted out, "I was going to ask Kerrick if there was any way to find out if someone called in the tip that got me arrested or if it really was just a random happening."

Kerrick looked up from his seat next to Mickey. "I could look into it. I don't know what I'll find out. Most of the time the calls come in anonymously, but I can look at the arrest record and talk to the arresting officer."

"I was going to ask Matt who he got the contact from, but he found his face in Keagan's fist and there was no chance to ask."

Everyone but Cole broke out into applause. He had no idea who Matt was. The others obviously felt like I did. Matt deserved a good ass-kicking for everything he put Holly through.

Kerrick turned his pumpkin and grinned. His was a failed attempt at a witch. The only thing he got right was the nose. At least I think it was the nose. It could have been a warty eye. Not sure.

Mickey was next. Standing proud, she displayed her work of art. Like Holly, she had carved into the orange flesh, but she carved out an elaborate ghost. I had to hand it to the women. They shamed us with their pumpkin carving skills.

I turned my pumpkin directly toward Holly. The last thing I wanted to cause was tears, but they slipped silently from her eyes, and I ran to her.

"I promised I would never cause you tears, and look what I've done. I hope you'll forgive me." My hands cupped her face. I dried her tears with the pads of my thumbs.

"They're tears of happiness. That was possibly the nicest thing anyone has done for me." She fisted my shirt and buried her face in my chest.

"I have no experience with this shit. I wanted to make you smile. I will always choose you."

Chapter 16

HOLLY

The weekend went by too fast. I got up with Keagan Sunday and helped care for the horses. There was something about hard work and sweat that made my body sing with satisfaction. The work was physically demanding, but the payoff was immediate. Clean stalls smelled more like hay than manure. Full haynets would be the joy of every horse who returned. Blue collar labor got a bad rep for no reason. I led a horse named Shoe into her stall and locked her in. She immediately went to eat, and I felt like I'd offered her a Michelin star experience.

Monday was exciting. I met with Joyce Cumberland, and she offered me a half-time position, interviewing terminal patients and their families. She also needed help contacting organizations to fulfill wishes. It sounded like something I'd enjoy while I waited for *my* wish to come true. What surprised me the most was that 'nonprofit' didn't mean no money. The salary she offered would rival my full-time pay from the hospital.

Mr. Conley allowed me to display our pumpkins in the entry to the facility. Of course, Killian's was banned. The pumpkins were numbered, and a jar was set nearby to collect the votes. I couldn't help cheating and looking to see who was winning. It appeared

Keagan had won several hearts besides mine. Everyone wanted to be chosen.

The rest of the week was nearly perfect, nearly because I hadn't heard from the board and Kerrick hadn't been able to turn up anything about my arrest. He was waiting for the actual records to be pulled from storage. Since the day he mentioned the stupidity of selling drugs on school grounds, I'd had a niggling suspicion I had, without a doubt, been set up.

Although I'd tried to contact Matt several times, he wasn't returning my calls. I imagined his bloody nose had something to do with it.

"Are you ready?" I asked. Keagan was running around his house, collecting pictures, whips, horseshoes, and anything else ranch related. "We're going to be late, and Mr. Hadaway doesn't do late."

"I'm coming." He ran to the mantel and pulled the picture of the horse dressed in ribbons. He dropped it into the box cradled in his arm and followed me out the door.

I'd invited him to the center to talk horses with Mr. Hadaway. I couldn't grant his wish to ride a horse or brand a cow. We both knew it wasn't possible, but I could bring in a cowboy who could spend hours talking about ranch life.

"Before we get there, I want to say thank you for making time to see a nice old man who has little time left." I reached for his hand and squeezed it. Keagan had become home for me. He was my safe place, and I couldn't imagine a life without him.

"We're a team, Holly." He pulled my hand to his mouth and let his lips hover over my knuckles. "I'll always be there when you need me," he whispered against my skin. His words warmed my heart, his lips heated my core. I began to calculate how long it would take us to visit with Mr. Hadley and get home to a bed. Too long.

"I love you." The words flowed freely. Life was fragile and uncertain. I'd learned the hard way to never miss an opportunity to tell someone how much I cared.

"Oh Holly, your love is a gift. Everything could disappear, and if you still loved me, I'd be happy." He made a hard right into the parking lot of Castle Care.

My heart played hopscotch in my chest. This was love, and it was amazing. For a second, I was angry I'd wasted so much time on a man not worthy of my love, but in the end I would have never appreciated Keagan if I hadn't experience Matt.

We exited his truck and headed inside. This was the first time he'd been there, so I proudly introduced him to everyone we passed. He stalled at the pumpkin display.

"When are we counting the votes?"

"Right after we visit with Mr. Hadaway." I pulled him behind me and led him down the hallway. He was like a kid with attention deficit disorder. He stopped to peek in rooms, gaze at art, and peruse the Wall of Fame. Finally, I got him to our intended destination.

"Mr. Hadaway, look who I brought." I walked into his room. The old man beamed like a child at the fair. From that moment forward, I didn't exist. Keagan shook his puffy hand and sat beside the man like they'd been friends forever. Another reason to love him more. He gave his all to everything he did.

I sat off to the side and listened to the men talk about breeding and branding. I'd always thought they heated an iron and burned their symbol into the hide of the animal, but I learned about cold branding today. A technique where dry ice and alcohol were used to freeze the branding irons before they were pressed against the hide. Keagan explained it was more humane, and they had fewer problems with infection.

Mr. Hadaway looked my way. "When are you branding that one?"

Keagan blushed. "I try to brand her every day."

When my mouth fell open, both men laughed until Mr. Hadaway began to choke. I rushed to his aid and tapped his back until his breathing was under control. I didn't want him to die laughing at my expense.

When our patient was looking spent, Keagan rose and said

farewell. He left a horseshoe on the nightstand and thanked Mr. Hadaway for his time.

"Wow." Outside the room, Keagan put the box he'd brought on the floor and pulled me into his arms. "What you do for these people is amazing. Thank you for allowing me to be a part of it. I'm floored." His kiss was soft and reverent.

"You made that man's day. Did you see how he lit up when you showed him the picture of Lucky Duck at the Derby? And when you brought out the whip and placed it in his hand? He looked twenty years younger."

"He obviously loved what he did. When you can do that, life is amazing. Are you loving what you're doing here?" He released me and bent over to pick up the box.

Did I love what I was doing? "Yes. I love being able to help heal a person's soul. I still feel like a nurse, only I heal people in a different way."

"No one will be able to take the nurse out of you. Now, let's go see who won the pumpkin contest so you can nurse my wounded ego."

While I went through the votes, Keagan hovered over my shoulder. Every time a vote came his way, he shouted, "Booyah" and fist-bumped the air.

"You think you're winning?" I stacked the votes in piles by number.

"No, I'm just happy that someone voted for mine."

"I voted for yours."

"How many times?"

"Not enough to let you win."

"That's just wrong."

When it was said and done, Mickey had won by three votes. My pumpkin came in second. Keagan's came in third. Cole and Kerrick tied for last. We piled the pumpkins into the truck and drove straight home. Halloween was tomorrow night, and although there wouldn't be tricksters looking for treats, we had planned to have a barbecue and bonfire.

When we got back to the ranch, Keagan went in search of Cole and Killian to make sure everything had run smoothly and finish the daily chores. I transferred the pumpkin to each person's cabin and lit the battery-operated candle. Everyone would come home to a little autumn cheer tonight.

As I approached my house, I noticed a white envelope peeking from the metal mailbox. The distinctive nursing board insignia jumped off the white background. My heart raced like a wild mustang escaping capture.

I'd run home every day and checked the box only to find it empty. Today it contained what I'd been seeking, and I was too frightened to look at it.

I dragged myself to the rocker and took a seat. Back and forth, I found a rhythm that soothed my nerves. The letter meant change. No matter what it said, something would continue and something would end.

Back and forth, back and forth, the creaking of the chair on the floorboards determined the pace of my breathing. Faster and faster I rocked. Faster and faster I breathed until I hyperventilated and had to stop.

Angry at myself for letting old habits resurface, I stood and pulled the letter from the box. The lid slammed closed, and I wondered if it was an omen.

I'd survived the death of my mother. I'd survived two years in prison. I'd survived betrayal. I would certainly survive whatever was in the envelope. That's what I told myself, but I wasn't sure I believed it. Too much was at stake.

Inside my home, I tossed the envelope on the table. This would take more than courage. It required liquid encouragement—possibly lots of liquid encouragement. After drinking a third of a bottle of cabernet, I ripped into the envelope and the words ripped into my heart.

Dear Ms. McGrath,

We regret to inform you that the request to reinstate your nursing license has been denied. After reviewing the file, we have determined it would not be in the best interests of the nursing board or the state of Colorado to restore your credentials...

Set Aside

The page became blurry after that. There was something about four letters, a history of drug problems, and a code that prohibited the licensing of a felon. The letter ended with a name, a number, and an apology.

I ripped the letter in half and threw it across the room. How could one mistake keep taking so much away from me? The room felt hot, the walls closed in. I couldn't breathe. I had to leave.

I yanked my jacket off the nearby hook and jerked the door open. It hit the wall and popped back, hitting me in the hind end as I left my home. I walked and cried until I'd run out of land and tears. When I looked around, I realized I'd walked to Keagan's bluff, the special place he came to think.

I sat on the ledge and let my legs hang over the edge. There was movement at the ranch, but everyone was so small, I couldn't identify anyone. From this perspective, everything seemed so inconsequential. The universe was spread out before me, and I was fixated on the smallest part of my life. The quiet floated around me.

I don't know why I ever thought I had a chance with the board. I don't know why they let me believe I did. My fate was set before I walked in and pleaded my case. What a waste of hope.

The whistle of a bird broke through my thoughts. The air was cold, the sun had set. A harvest moon hung low in the sky, throwing off an eerie orange glow.

"Hey," Keagan's soft voice crooned behind me. "I was worried about you." He sat next to me and covered my shaking body with his jacket.

"How did you find me?" I curled into his side, seeking his warmth—his strength.

"I saw you walking earlier, and when I got to your place and you were gone, I knew where to look." He didn't press for information. He offered comfort.

"It's been a tough afternoon. I got my letter, and it wasn't good." Tucked in the protection of his arms, I cried buckets of tears.

Keagan didn't try to convince me it would be okay. He held me and hugged me and kissed me.

He gave me the courage to stand up and dust off my boots. I'd been through worse. I'd come out scarred but alive.

"Mom used to say when one door closes..." The sentence faded as I pictured my mother saying it.

"Another opens," Keagan filled in.

"No. When one door closes, climb out the window and meet me in the bar." In spite of the somber situation, I managed a giggle.

"Your mother was a smart woman. Let's go home, and I'll pour you a drink." He walked me down the well-worn path. All the while, I kept seeing the reference to four letters and a history of drug problems pop in my head. *What the fuck were they talking about?* Come Monday, I was getting some answers.

Chapter 17

KEAGAN

The letter was devastating news to Holly, but I think deep down she expected it. When I got her home, I undressed her and put her in a hot bath. She was cold to her core. While she soaked, I built a fire and poured her a glass of wine. We sat in silence and watched the flames flicker and the firelight dance off the walls. On any other night this would have been romantic, but tonight it was a way for her to cope.

After a cup of soup, I lit her gardenia candle and tucked her into bed. She stayed in my arms all night. Hers wasn't a peaceful sleep. She tossed and turned until I pulled her close to my chest and held her tight.

When I rose for morning chores, she had finally given in to a deep slumber. I scribbled a note telling her I loved her and I'd be back at nine with breakfast.

Killian and Cole were already in the stables when I arrived.

"Everything okay?" Killian asked. He must have seen the concern on my face.

"Nope, but it will be. It'll just take some time." I grabbed the pitchfork and starting mucking out the stables. The work was a welcome relief, a way to release my pent-up stress. "Holly permanently lost her license."

"Shit," Cole said as he shoveled dung beside me.

"Yep. It's a setback for her, but she'll be okay. She's tougher than she looks."

Killian was silent as he tossed fresh pellets on the floor and watered them down. He shut off the hose and came to stand in front of me. "Do we need to kick someone's ass? I could go for a good ass-kicking."

"Not yet, but I'll let you know." I left Cole and Killian at eight forty-five and returned to the house. My girl was still in bed. She loved pancakes, so that's what I whipped up and delivered straight to her bed.

She told me she wasn't hungry, but I fed her bite after bite until I was satisfied she'd eaten enough. She'd had a bowl of soup and nothing else the previous day. After her two pancakes, she curled up and went back to sleep. That's how the next several hours went. I came back at lunch and made her eat a grilled cheese sandwich and tomato soup. She rolled in a ball and escaped back into sleep. By five, I'd had enough of her hiding under the covers. I pulled her from the bed and carried her to the bathroom.

She was dressed in the same Hot Chili Peppers T-shirt I'd seen the first night I'd stayed with her. Her hair was a mess a rat would have loved to nest in. I was worried.

"Holly, we're showering, then we're joining everyone for the bonfire and BBQ. Don't think anyone out there is going to let you sulk the whole weekend. You're a McGrath-McKinley, and we don't sulk. We conquer." I stripped her naked and pulled her into the shower with me.

"I'm not a McKinley." She stood under the water and let it run over her.

"I beg to differ. I've deposited enough DNA in your beautiful body to make you one. Now snap out of it." I shampooed her hair and cleaned her body from top to toes. When we stepped out the shower, I didn't take the time to dry her. I knew how to make her come alive, and for the next hour I did.

Set Aside

I licked her dry and kissed her wounded heart. I told her the truth about herself. She was remarkable and capable of anything. I reminded her how much people needed her—Mr. Hadaway, Jasper Felding, and Mrs. Lakewood's lives were changed because of her. I was changed because of her.

"I need you, Holly, don't leave me alone." I buried my face against her neck.

"I'm not going anywhere." And my Holly was back.

She insisted on wearing my shirt to the cookout. She said my scent comforted her and reminded her she wasn't alone. I was happy to let her wear my clothes; she looked a damn sight sexier in them than I did.

We joined the others by the firepit where Cole was building an inferno.

"Don't you dare burn yourself tonight," I warned. "Holly isn't fixin' you up if you do." Cole laughed and threw another log on the fire.

Roland was manning the barbecue, while Kerrick was popping caps off beers. In the distance, Mickey and Killian were carrying side dishes from the main house. A few flakes of snow were falling from the sky. We'd picked a fine day to socialize outside.

Everyone knew Holly had lost her license and the subject was off limits. We were a ragtag bunch, but we were a family, and we'd take care of each other. Cole had yet to earn his place, but he was fast becoming indispensable.

"How in the hell did I lose the pumpkin carving contest?" Kerrick asked between bites of burger. "Mine was the scariest."

Holly nearly choked on her dog. "No one knew what you carved. Next time, be clear about your intentions." She'd been sitting silently in my lap the whole evening. Apparently, a beer had loosened her up. I motioned for Kerrick to toss me another. Instead, he rose to his feet, grabbed several beers, and put a fresh one in each of our hands.

"I want to propose a toast. Months ago I picked up a skinny-assed, pain in the rear slip of a woman from the side of the road. She had my attention by the time we had reached the grocery store.

She had my heart the minute we walked down the personal hygiene aisle. Holly was talking about making my intentions clear." Kerrick dropped to his knees in front of Mickey. "Mickey Mercer, I intend to make you mine."

"Oh, holy shit..." Killian rose from his chair and paced in front of the fire. One would have thought he was the one proposing.

Kerrick pulled something from his pocket and slipped it on Mickey's finger. "Will you be mine forever?"

"Hell yes," Mickey shouted loud enough for people in El Paso County to hear.

Holly jumped from my lap and raced to her friend. They held hands and jumped around in circles. The guys stood by the fire and watched. After a few slaps on the back, the men were back to eating. The girls went straight into wedding planning. Mickey looked longingly at the ring on her finger. Holly looked at me. I halfway wished it were me who'd stepped up to the plate tonight.

I could have kissed my brother. He'd given Holly the perfect distraction. Something to focus on besides her loss.

"M and M will still work for the name." Cole smiled. He looked as if he'd figured out something amazing, like the cure for cancer.

"Yes, it would," Mickey said. "However, I was thinking of changing it up. You know how books sometimes have taglines? Well, what about The Second Chance Ranch? This land has given all of us hope. It's changed lives." Mickey looked at Holly. Even I could feel the love between the two women. They had been through hell together, and this ranch was a safe place to land and would continue to be for several other women.

Killian piped in first. "I think S and M ranch sounds more intriguing, but second chance works." Kerrick was quick with the punch to his arm.

Roland was the next to offer up something. "It sounds perfect. So...Kerrick gets Mickey, Keagan gets Holly, where does that leave the rest of us? Who's falling next? And what's her name? I want to be prepared."

Holly brightened at the mention of the girls left behind. "Megan is next. She's had a tough life. She's definitely not for Killian. You'd scare that poor girl to death with your intensity."

"I'm not intense. I'm...passionate."

"That's why I'm taking my fiancée home and to bed. I'm feeling passionate. You all have a good night." Kerrick picked Mickey up and carried her to the house. No one expected to see them for a while.

The rest of us hung out until the embers died down. Cole took the leftovers to his house. Killian banked the fire, and I went home with Holly and tried to ignite a spark in her.

Once she was heated up, we made love several times. We lay sweaty and sated, our limbs intertwined. I was just dozing when she said, "Shit, I forgot to ask your brother about the arrest record."

Chapter 18

HOLLY

The morning sun slipped through the tiny slit in the curtains. Why was it the only place that let in sun was the place that was perfectly lined up with my eyes? I threw back the covers and went in search of coffee.

We had stayed in Keagan's cabin last night. The room smelled of his citrus and pine cologne and leather. That scent stayed with me until I reached the kitchen, where I found a pot of hot coffee and a note.

Morning Sweetheart,

Grab a mug and come out to the stables. The farrier is coming today. Shoeing can be interesting. I love you.

K

I pulled a pair of panties from Keagan's drawer. Our clothes were cohabiting in both houses; probably because he had a way of stealing my panties, and I had a way of borrowing his shirts. I threw on my jeans from yesterday and pulled a clean shirt from his closet. The poor man had very little to wear these days, but I preferred him in nothing.

The minute my toast popped up, I grabbed it along with my mug of coffee and headed toward the stables. I didn't give a damn

Set Aside

about horseshoeing. I gave a damn about Keagan. He had really helped me get through the shock of losing my license. He held me, loved me, and listened. He gave everything and took nothing.

When I arrived, the stables were a hive of activity. The weekends were always busy. People came to ride their horses. Cole was giving roping lessons, Mickey was working with a teen on barrel racing techniques, and Killian was in the paddock training one of the rescues.

My man stood by the split-rail fence and was talking to Kerrick. The men were close. I hoped someday I'd have a herd of children that took care of each other the way the McKinleys took care of each other. Hell, I dreamed I'd have a brood of boys that looked just like Keagan, with dark hair and hazel eyes. If we had a girl, she'd be stunning. Her father's eyes and her long dark hair would turn every boy's head in town. Her daddy would be using that whip he was showing Mr. Hadaway. In my mind, our future was charted.

Roland was near the end of the stalls talking to the farrier, an older man with hair the color of a marshmallow and skin the color of pink bubblegum. Since Keagan wanted me to see how a horse was shoed, I walked in that direction.

Why did horses need shoes anyway? They had hooves. Wasn't that enough? A silly thought crossed my mind. Bare feet weren't enough for me. I had boots, sandals, heels, and sneakers. I suppose Target had become my farrier.

"Hey, Holly." Roland gave me a hug and introduced me to Mike Bohanon. Mike was shoeing Brandy, one of the rescues. She was as black as the midnight sky, with a perfect white diamond on her forehead. She didn't seem to be bothered by the man who had her front hoof between his legs.

Shoeing was an interesting process, much like a pedicure for a horse. The farrier clipped and scraped at her hoof before fitting a metal shoe to the bottom. "Does that hurt her?" I asked while he drove the nails into her hoof.

"Well, I've shoed thousands of horses, and they've never complained." He tapped in the last nail and moved on to the next hoof.

The removal of her old shoes fascinated me. Roland picked out the nails and handed the worn horseshoe to me, telling me to keep it upright so my luck wouldn't spill out. It would have been easy to believe I was out of luck after yesterday, but a glance around the stables told me differently. My luck hadn't left me, it had changed.

When Mike was finished with Brandy, I stayed behind and talked to her. She nudged me the way Brody did Keagan. I thought it was an act of endearment, but maybe Brody was actually telling Keagan to take a hike, and maybe Brandy was telling me the same.

"She likes you." Keagan's hands slipped around my waist, his chin rested on my head. "She has good taste."

"How do you know she likes me?" I reached up to trace her white diamond with my finger.

"There aren't any hoof marks on your face." He chuckled against my neck.

"You're awful. No, really, how can you tell?" Brandy stuck her muzzle in my hair. I could hear her inhale my scent, or maybe that was Keagan.

"First, she came to you. You didn't coax her, you stood by her stall, and she approached. You didn't give her a treat, and she stayed. She trusts you. And it's a good thing, because she's yours. Killian picked her out for you." His grin stretched from earlobe to earlobe.

I stopped breathing. They were giving me a horse of my own. Diesel would no longer have to put up with my mixed signals and my poor seat. Brandy and I would train together.

"Really? She's mine?" I swung around and tackled my man.

"Yep. All yours." He caught me as I flew at him and wrapped my legs around his waist. I knew the gift was from everyone, but he was the first person I'd come in contact with. I planned to make my rounds and kiss everyone I could catch. Keagan wouldn't be happy, but I would be.

In spite of everything I'd lost, I had come out ahead. Sure, there were a few mysteries to solve before I could bury the past, but I'd get on those tomorrow. Today was all about hope and family, and I wanted to get to know my horse better.

Set Aside

"Can I ride her?"

"Mike assures me she's good. A short ride on her new shoes will work out just fine. We need to fit her with a saddle first." Still carrying me, he walked us both into the tack room and closed the door. "I've been dying to get you in here." He let me slide down his body before he captured my mouth in a quick but hot kiss.

"Why?" There were saddles, pads, harnesses, and every other thing a horse would need, but nothing that needed our combined attention.

He picked up a heavy wooden horse and pressed it against the door.

"The smell of leather does something for me." He threw a few horse blankets on the dirt floor and laid me down. We made love in the tack room.

I swear I developed a new love for the smell of leather and dirt.

"We're going to have to put a lock on that door." I lifted up on my elbows and looked toward the only thing keeping us from prying eyes. There wasn't a cowboy on this ranch that couldn't move that door with a single push. I only hoped no one would need a lead, a pad, or anything else.

"You like making love in the tack room?" He helped me dress between kisses. His lips were so distracting, I almost stripped myself naked again so we could have a repeat.

"Yes."

"I'll get a lock."

"When?"

"Tomorrow."

"Perfect."

"Yes, you are."

Keagan picked out a saddle for Brandy. Who knew so much went into a ride? When we left the tack room, there wasn't a person connected to the ranch who didn't know what we were up to. I wanted to hide in shame, but I didn't. I was becoming a cowgirl, and they were made from tougher stuff, so I pulled my shoulders back and walked past the knowing grins.

Kerrick followed us to Brandy's stall.

"I got the report back, and the interesting thing about it was the police were tipped off the day before the deal went down. Who knew where the meeting was?" he asked.

I knew of one person for certain, but I had a sneaking suspicion he wasn't the one to call in the tip.

"Matt."

"The call came from an anonymous woman." Kerrick rubbed the stubble on his jaw. No one said a word, but we all knew it was Carla. Just one more thing to deal with tomorrow.

The ride on Brandy was exactly what I needed to temper my fury. Horses were very perceptive. I didn't want us to get off to a bad start, so I set aside my anger and enjoyed a perfect moment with my horse and my man.

KEAGAN WAS UP EARLY, and so was I. I insisted on taking care of my horse on my own. I had an eight o'clock meeting with Joyce to discuss several patients I'd be meeting with next week, so I didn't have all day to whisper sweet words to Brandy, but she seemed to like that I brushed her and let her run loose in the paddock with Darcy's Pride. The two horses were well-suited to each other.

I kissed Keagan goodbye and hugged him extra long. Concern filled his eyes.

"You going to be all right?" I swear he had X-ray vision capable of seeing into my soul.

"Of course. I have you and all of this." I spread my arms and twirled in a circle. He appeared to relax.

I didn't tell him I'd be stopping at the board to pick up the letters that were written on my behalf. I was entitled to a copy of my file, and I intended to get it. Today.

I also didn't tell him I'd be stopping by the hospital to get the last piece to the puzzle. Matt was going to tell me who he got the contact information from, even if I had to hunt him down to get it. I already knew; I just needed it confirmed.

When I arrived at Castle Care, there was an ambulance in the driveway. By the size of the sheet-covered body the paramedics wheeled out, I knew it was Mr. Hadaway. His loss choked me up. It was just a few days ago he'd talked horses with Keagan. I'd never seen him so happy and at peace. Keagan gave him that, and I had given him Keagan.

I swiped at the tears that ran down my face and shored up my courage before I walked inside. This was my new calling. I'd make sure everyone here knew they had value beyond their final breath.

Joyce and I had coffee and discussed the cases she was working on. She jumped from her chair when I informed her I was going to be a permanent hire. She promised me full-time soon, but I wasn't for that. I liked the way my life was going.

I could work for Finishing Touches two or three days a week. That would give me plenty of time to volunteer, help at the ranch, and spend time with Keagan. My life felt balanced and comfortable for the first time in years.

Thirty minutes later, I was at the licensing board, picking up the file. The reference to four letters ate at me. I knew about three, which meant the fourth had to come from Carla, and I was interested in what she had to say.

I sat in my Jeep and read the letters one by one. Maggie was kind with her words and praised me for being honest and fair. Dr. Sturgeous made me sound like a modern day Florence Nightingale. Even Matt was generous with his praise. But when I read the final letter, I was outraged.

To Whom It May Concern:

I have known Holly McGrath for many years. We attended nursing school together and worked together for the last several years. I have a nine-year history with her. In all the time I've known her, she has had issues with substance abuse.

Prior to her incarceration, she was the shift supervisor in the emergency room. This position gave her access to a plethora of controlled substances. It didn't surprise me that she was arrested for dealing drugs as the cabinets came up empty on more than one occasion.

I can't with an honest heart recommend the renewal of her license. Sincerely,

Carla Worthington – Shift Supervisor, Denver General Hospital

To say I was stunned was an understatement. Why would she go to such great lengths to destroy my life? I jammed my Jeep into gear and sped to Denver General Hospital.

Maggie was at the intake desk when I arrived.

"What's wrong? You look like an angry hornet." She grabbed the letter I shoved through the security slot and read it.

"No fucking way." She threw her hand over her mouth, but it was too late; she had already drawn the attention of several people in the ER. She passed my letter around like a cheerleader on prom night. It wasn't something I would have shared, but I was too angry to care who knew at this point.

"Where's Dr. Becker?" I took several long breaths and waited.

"I just saw him in the cafeteria." She pulled my letter out of a nurse's hand and shoved it back through the slot. "He's not alone."

"Good." I stormed down the hallway to the elevator. When that was taking too long, I shoved open the stairwell door and took the steps two at a time. I was clenching my fists so tightly, the letter in my hand nearly disintegrated.

There were a lot of people in the cafeteria; not shocking for lunchtime. I scanned the perimeter of the room. The outside was where Matt would have been. He liked the view it gave him. I always thought it was about watching his colleagues, and in a way it was. But it was actually about *watching* his colleagues. Their tits, asses, and long legs were all he was interested in.

When I saw him in the corner with Carla, I didn't waste a breath. I was hovering over their table in seconds.

"Holly, what a surprise. Done slumming?" I wanted to slap the crap out of that man, but it looked like his nose might have just healed. The bump on the bridge would be a permanent reminder of his run-in with Keagan. He didn't need a second one to remind him of me.

"Shut up, Matt. I'm here for one thing only." Off to my right was Carla. She didn't look comfortable. She kept staring at the wrinkled paper in my hand. She knew. I could tell by the trapped animal look she gave me.

"I'll go." She stood, but I pushed her back into her seat.

Set Aside

"You'll stay," I yelled. I was drawing attention from many people, but I didn't care. This was going to end today.

"When you gave me the contact for the pot pusher, who did you get it from?" Matt looked around the room. "Tell me," I screamed.

He wasn't used to that kind of rage coming from me, and I imagined it frightened him. I was no longer an angry hornet. I was the nest, and I'd been poked at far too long.

"Carla...Carla gave it to me." There was nothing like having a man throw you under the bus.

"I did not," she countered.

They argued back and forth for several minutes until Carla gave up and Matt won.

I tossed the letter at Matt and watched his face fall as he read it. Carla's face contorted, and her cheeks blazed ember red.

"Why?" I stared her down.

She was silent.

"Why?" I repeated and pounded my fist on the table.

Carla got up and surged forward. She pushed against my chest, and I stumbled backward, falling into a table of mesmerized diners.

"Because you were in the way." Her voice could have raised the ceiling. It raised the hairs on my arms.

"You tossed my life away because you wanted him?" I pointed toward Matt who was watching with rapt attention. "You could have had him."

"I do have him." Her voice was smug and condescending.

"And my job?"

"You stopped my upward mobility. I'd never get promoted while you were around."

It all made sense. She took everything away because she couldn't compete. She was willing to sacrifice my life to have her own.

"You know what, Carla? I feel sorry for you. You slept with my fiancé, which isn't a surprise because he slept with everyone. You provided the contact so I could get weed for my cancer-stricken mother. Then you called in a tip to let the police know where it was going down." Several gasps came from the crowd.

Her eyes went huge. She opened her mouth to speak, but only the word "I" came out.

I gave her a five-finger stop. "Shut the fuck up." By that time, we were surrounded by onlookers. "You didn't stop there; you made sure I'd never come back. You slandered me to the hospital board with your letter. And you know what? I could get over everything except for the fact that you cheated me out of the last moments with my dying mother."

It all boiled down to that moment. Something took over, and I had no control. I curled my fingers tight and wrapped my thumb around my balled up fist. I struck. One powerful thrust to her nose, and she was out. Her body collapsed on the ground.

It was surprising that in a room full of physicians, no one came to her aid. The blood poured from her nose onto the speckled industrial floor. The crack I'd heard told me I'd broken that pert little stub she held up in the air. She'd be sporting two black eyes and a wonky nose for some time.

I pulled my letter off the table and began to walk toward the door. I felt like Moses as people cut a wide path for me.

Keagan was right—sometimes violence was justified.

Chapter 19

KEAGAN

I was tucking Brody into his stall when my phone vibrated. The number was not listed.

"Hello."

"Keagan," Holly cried. "I'm in jail."

I've heard people say the world fell out from under their feet. I'd imagined it was a figure of speech, but when I heard her voice, my knees buckled and I found myself on them in the middle of the staff stables.

Mickey had just moved Brandy to a new stall so Holly could be closer to her horse. Kerrick was standing off to the side on the phone. Killian was already at my side while Cole stepped in to finish with Brody.

"What do you mean you're in jail?" I didn't recognize my voice. It wavered like a bad connection. My throat closed, and my head began to pound.

Everyone was silenced when they heard me talking.

"Sweetheart, where are you?" I tried a soft approach, trying to coax the information out of her.

She told me the county jail, and I whispered for Mickey to get

Kerrick on it right away. She hadn't given me enough time to get the details, but she was being held for assault and battery. By the time she hung up, I wasn't sure who she'd hit. My ego hoped it was Matt, but my gut told me it was Carla.

Everyone piled into their trucks and raced toward the jail. When we arrived, the only person they allowed in to see her was Kerrick, and it killed me. He flashed his badge and said he was conducting an interview, and they took him right in.

Helpless, I paced the lobby. I'd promised to take care of her, and there was nothing I could do to help.

I rushed to Kerrick when he came out.

"Is she okay?"

He dropped his head. "She's okay, but she's upset that she put herself in this position. I told her you loved her, and we'd be working on getting her out soon." He reached for Mickey, who was standing nearby and pulled her to his side. How long would it be before I had Holly back in my arms?

"I need to see her. Can't you trade a favor or something?" I pleaded with my big brother. Weren't they supposed to be able to fix everything?

"I traded that favor just now. I had no business butting into her case." He'd done all he could, so I was grateful.

"What's next?" The heaviness in my shoulders made me sag.

"I'm heading to the hospital to talk to a few people. I'll let you know if I find out anything that can change the outcome. As it stands now, she's an ex-con, and they're not going to go easy on her." Kerrick patted my back, but I brushed him off. I didn't want to be placated. I needed a solution.

"I'm going with you." I turned and started for the door.

"No." He sounded like our father. He said it, and he meant it. There would be no arguments. "I don't need both of you in jail. Take Mickey home, and wait there for me."

I did as he said, not because I wanted to, but because he was best suited to handle the crisis. I dropped off Mickey at her door and went straight to Holly's cabin. I needed to be close to her, and if

Set Aside

I couldn't do that, I'd be close to her things. I curled up in her bed with my boots on and buried my face in her pillow. What in the hell would I do if she got sent back to prison?

Chapter 20

HOLLY

The first time they slammed the metal doors, I was terrified. I had no idea what to expect. I'd heard stories about the dangers of incarceration. Shanking and rape. Beatings and starvation. Those weren't the things that frightened me now. I'd been down this road, and although I'd traveled it before, I had more on the line this time, and I was petrified.

There was no way to change the outcome last time. My mom was guaranteed to die, whether I was in jail or not. This time Keagan would be lost to me, and so would all the dark-haired, hazel-eyed children I'd dreamed about.

Mickey and Kerrick would get married, and I'd be in jail instead of standing beside my best friend.

Killian would eventually find a girl who'd challenge him, and I'd miss all the fireworks.

Cole would undoubtedly need first aid, and there would be no one to administer it.

And Roland would keep bringing strays, whether they were horses, cats, or whatever he rounded up, and I'd miss out on loving the orphans.

Set Aside

Sadly, my horse would belong to someone else, and she'd lose her trust in me because I had abandoned her.

I lowered my head and sobbed.

"You okay, darlin'?"

I swiped at my tears. "Yes, I'll be okay." It was easy to say the words, hard to believe them.

"What ya in for, darlin'?" She picked at her jagged nails.

"I punched someone in the face." I eyed my knuckles; they were swollen, but I hadn't broken the skin. That was a positive at least. I wouldn't be carrying a disease for the rest of my life, courtesy of Carla.

"Did she deserve it?" She bit off a hangnail and spit it on the floor.

"Yes, she did. I broke her nose."

"Well then, doll, do your time and be proud it was worth it. I got caught in the alleyway behind a hotel."

"Was it worth it?" I flexed my fingers, trying to keep them mobile.

"Hell no. Worst lay of my life, and the bastard shortchanged me, but this ain't my first rodeo. I'll make bail soon."

At the mention of a rodeo, I became a blubbering mess. The hooker got up and sat next to me to offer comfort. She adjusted the skirt that had ridden up to show her goodies. How she managed to get five inches of spandex to cover her bottom was a mystery.

I leaned into her shoulder and cried. Her dime store perfume burned my nose, but her soothing words helped get me through the next hour.

"McGrath." I popped up at the sound of my name. "Lawyer's here." The guard opened the cage and led me out.

In a small room, I sat and waited. It wasn't like the movies. I wasn't handcuffed to a table. My ankles weren't tethered together. I sat in a metal chair in front of a metal table and waited.

A man with a cue ball head and ZZ Top beard approached. He pulled out paper and a pen and sat across from me. He didn't appear lawyerly. He looked comfortable in his khakis and collared shirt. Just goes to show you, you shouldn't judge people by the length of their beard. I'd have pegged him to be a New Age tree hugger, or possibly a dispensary owner, but never a lawyer.

"I'm Rob McNally. Your lawyer."

"Who sent you?"

"Let's see...there was Cole, Kerrick, Killian, Mickey, Keagan, and a horse named Brandy." His pearly whites barely showed through his sagebrush face.

"Wow." I was overwhelmed by the love that was pouring out to me. I'd had a court-appointed lawyer the first time. With Mom's treatments, we couldn't afford anything more.

"I don't know how I'll pay you, but I will." His brow lifted.

I wondered if I'd just screwed myself. I suppose the last thing you should tell your lawyer is you're broke.

"This is a family thing. Cole's my brother. I'm here pro bono."

"Cole?"

"Yep, he's my baby bro, and when he calls, I come." He fanned out a few pages and began. "So, let's get started. Ms. Worthington claims you attacked her, but there are eyewitnesses who say she pushed you first and you were defending yourself. Tell me your truth."

I told him the story from start to finish. His expression didn't give anything away. Hell, I could hardly see his face through his whiskers. I'd have had a devil of a time meshing out an expression.

"How is Keagan?"

"Pissed."

"Can you tell him I love him?"

"Yep." He pushed his papers into a pile and carefully placed them in the satchel he carried in. "Carla is going for felony aggravated assault. We'll try to get the charges dismissed because she attacked first. The worst scenario is, you're looking at a year or two for second-degree assault. Your previous felony isn't going to help. The best case would be a dismissal or for the defendant to drop the charges. I'll be in touch."

My stomach and hope sank to the floor. Rob gathered his things and knocked on the door to leave. I was taken back to my empty

Set Aside

cell. The hooker had it right; she'd made bail, and I was once again alone.

Over the next two days, I had three additional cellmates. The first was a drunken woman named Tammy, who kept flashing the guards in the hopes they'd bring her a drink. They obliged with water, but nothing stronger. She wasn't happy. It would appear she wasn't a stranger to the system. Several of the guards knew her by name, and they all chatted like old friends. Once she was sober, they let her loose.

My next roomie was a young woman named Beth. She was in for a DUI. Her first. Hopefully, her last. She stayed about three hours before her parents bailed her out.

Bail wasn't a luxury I was offered.

My most recent cellmate was a woman named Sarah, but I knew her as Trixie. She'd been in cell block C when I was there. When she wasn't turning tricks, she was selling drugs. She was definitely going back to the Denver Women's Correctional Facility. Trafficking was a felony, and when she said she'd had over a pound on her, I felt bad for her.

We lay in our bunks and talked about the women of cell block C. She'd only been free for a week, so she gave me the lowdown on everyone. By the time we tired, I felt like I'd been to a reunion.

I closed my eyes and thought of where they'd bunk me when I returned to prison. I silently prayed for cell block C.

"McGrath." The guard's voice echoed through the cell. I bolted up and banged my head on the bunk above me.

I jumped from the thin mattress and walked to the bars. He slid the gate open and led me out. Bummer that I got Officer Grumpy. Each time I asked him a question, he ignored me. If I wasn't afraid of getting in more trouble, I would have stopped walking and demanded he tell me where I was headed.

He turned me over to a female officer who escorted me to a locker where my clothes were stored. Being given my clothes was odd, given that I'd been in an orange jumpsuit for two days, a sign I was long-term.

"What's happening?"

"Charges were dropped; you're being released." She opened the locker and handed me my clothes.

I couldn't quite process her statement, so I asked for a repeat.

"Charges dropped; we can't hold you."

I'd never changed so quickly in my life. I wanted out of there as fast as I could manage. Something in the back of my mind said they'd made a mistake, and I was afraid they'd figure it out if I didn't hurry. I shoved my jumpsuit into the laundry basket and followed the officer to a side door that opened to the outside.

The sun was peeking above buildings, and the slightest shade of yellow danced across the horizon. It had stormed while I was in jail. White fluffy snow coated the dirty asphalt; everything appeared fresh and new.

I scanned the parking lot looking for someone I knew. My heart twisted when I didn't see anyone waiting for me. On my second glance, I spotted a sexy cowboy leaning against his black truck. His hat pulled low over his brow gave him a mysterious look.

I bolted down the steps and into his arms.

"You came for me."

"Sweetheart, I told you before, I would have waited for you, and I did. Now let's get the hell out of here before they change their minds."

We hopped in the car and sped away. After a few blocks, he pulled the truck over and hauled me into his lap, where he kissed me long and hard. When his hand slid up my shirt to cup my breast, I stopped him.

"I'm not getting out of jail and going straight back for indecent exposure. Take me home." And we raced in that direction.

"Did you get the lock?" I asked as the landscape sped past us.

"What?" He glanced at me, then turned his attention to the road.

"Tack room, or bedroom?"

"You aren't leaving our room. I can't afford to let you out of my sight. After I make use of our bed, I plan to make love to you in every location possible. I'd even try Brody's back if I thought he'd cooperate."

Set Aside

"Hmm, that sounds interesting." I slid my body against his and rubbed his thigh from his knee to the crotch of his pants. He stopped my hand after the first pass.

"Do that again, and to hell with indecent exposure; I'll join you in jail." It would be shocking if we made it in the door, given the state of his arousal. "By the way, you've been sick for three days. Joyce is looking forward to your return next Monday."

During this whole time, I'd never given my job a single thought. Only my family had mattered. Mickey and the McKinleys, Cole, and Roland, and now Rob, but most of all I thought about Keagan and how, in a short period of time, he'd made me feel whole again.

He tore up the gravel as we sped toward his cabin. Once he threw the truck in park, we were out the door and running toward his room. Our clothes were flung in every direction on our way.

When he sank himself inside of me, I cried; only this time, he knew I was happy. He kissed my tears as we made love, and he told me how many ways he would love me forever. When I screamed his name, he slumped on top of me and let the emotion cover us both.

"Keagan?"

He rolled to his side and looked at me. His eyes were sexy, and his lids hung low.

"What, sweetheart?" He kissed my forehead, then my nose.

I stalled for a moment, then realized if I didn't ask now, I'd never have the courage later. Those days in jail reminded me that life was uncertain, and I needed to capture every moment. I promised myself if I got out, I would claim what I wanted. What was mine.

"I know I'll never love anyone but you." My heart raced like a spooked horse. What I was about to say would change my life. "Will you be mine forever?"

He smiled big and wide. "You're asking me to marry you?"

"Yes."

He pulled his left hand between us and looked at his empty finger. "What, no ring?"

"I'll get you one."

"When?"

"Tomorrow."

"Perfect."

"Yes, you are."

THE VERY NEXT DAY, Keagan and I gathered the masses and went to City Hall. Colorado didn't require a blood test to tie the knot. I didn't need ribbons, lace, and cake that normal brides craved. I needed Keagan, and I needed to know he was mine forever.

We exchanged vows in front of our family. We did things a bit backward. We had a shotgun wedding, bought our rings, and then went on our first real off-the-ranch date. He took me to Trevi's Steakhouse, where we celebrated our life to come and planned our brood of brown-haired, hazel-eyed children.

Curious minds wanted to know, and Keagan explained how Kerrick played good cop/bad cop. He informed Carla she was being investigated for filing a false report with the nursing board. After he gave a detailed description of what her prison cell would look like, he explained how the charges could be dropped if she did the right thing. Carla asked him for a ride to the police station.

My mom used to say bad things happened to good people, but good things happened to good people, too. And sometimes bad people did the right thing, and that was good.

NEXT UP IS *SET IN* Stone

A Sneak Peek at Set in Stone

Three years ago, I had landed in prison for vehicular manslaughter. Today, I stood on the frigid sidewalk outside the Denver Women's Correctional Facility. For a fleeting moment, I wished I were locked up again. Was it wrong to crave the predictability of my past? The day Tyler lost his life, I'd lost a lot, too. At least I'd know how to survive when I'd been Tyler's hostage or a prisoner of the state. Today, I was stepping into a new world full of possibilities, and it scared the hell out of me.

My teeth chattered while the wind whistled across the blank slate of freshly fallen snow. With one hundred and eighty-six dollars to my name, and my only outfit a prison-gifted pair of sweatpants and a long-sleeved T-shirt, I was lacking in everything except hope.

The sound of the horn hit me before the vehicle could be seen, but the minute the blue truck did a donut in front of me, my life became brighter. The girls had arrived. In seconds, the truck was turned off, and Mickey and Holly were wrapped around me. Their loving arms reinforced my desire to push forward despite my dreadful circumstances. I had never been so grateful to see their goofy grins and feel their warm embrace.

"Shit, Megan, is that all they gave you to wear?" Mickey ran her hands up and down my near-frozen arms. She pulled the too-big T-shirt up to cover my exposed shoulder.

"I'm no longer their problem." For the first time in a long time, I was free. Free to choose, free to live, free to love and be loved. In all my years, I'd never been free or loved.

"Put this on." Holly took off her jacket and draped it over my shoulders. Her warmth seeped into me like hot syrup on pancakes.

"Thank you. S…s…sorry," I chattered. "I'm such a pain."

Would I ever feel like I wasn't a scab on someone's arm? My therapist told me I had to stop the negative feedback that played in an endless loop in my mind, but I'd been programmed to feel worthless. Mom had planted the message on my eighteenth birthday when she'd left my suitcase on the front porch with a note that said *good luck with your life*. What mother says *peace out* as soon as their child can no longer earn them EBT from the welfare department? The next sets of messages were *felt* loud and clear. Tyler reinforced my feelings of worthlessness each time he raised his voice and his fist.

Mickey stood in front of me and pulled my chin forward, giving me no option but to look at her. "Megan, stop it." She glowered at me while Holly looked over Mickey's shoulder with sympathy swimming in her eyes. "You're not a pain. You're a strong independent woman. You can do this. Don't fall back into old habits." She pulled me into her arms and squeezed me tight. "We're your friends, and we'll always be here for you whether you're a pain or not, and today you're not."

"That's right." Holly stepped to Mickey's side and looked down at my rolled-up sweatpants, prison sneakers, and baggy shirt. "There's no way you're spending another minute in that hideous outfit. Mickey and I owe you Christmas presents, so let's go shopping." She clapped her hands and danced around me. Her enthusiasm was enough for the three of us.

"I have some money." I dipped my hand into my bra and pulled out the check I'd received that morning for two years of laundry service. "I don't want to be a charity case."

"Oh, shush." Holly wove her fingers through mine and pulled

A Sneak Peek at Set in Stone

me toward the passenger side of the truck. "Get in. I'm freezing." She wrapped her sweater-covered arms around herself and shivered. "Today, your money isn't needed."

Once in the truck, the girls got all chatty about life at the ranch. Mickey got soft looking when she spoke of Kerrick and all he'd done for her.

"Without Kerrick and his brothers, I'd have nothing. The McKinleys saved my ranch, and I'm paying that kindness forward. You're the recipient." Mickey twisted the key to the old beat-up truck. The engine stuttered, then rumbled to life. "When you can, you'll do the same. Natalie and Robyn are getting out soon, and they'll need help too."

The fabulous five was what we called ourselves. Who would have thought that five women who came from such different walks of life could become best friends? Soon Natalie and Robyn would be released, and I'd be the third set of arms wrapped around them. Holly draped her arm over my shoulders and pulled me to her side. In her arms, I felt safe, cozy, and valued. These were the sisters I'd never had. The family I'd always wanted.

Holly whispered against my hair, "Mickey, Kerrick, and Keagan were my saviors." She sighed her contentment. "The beginning is going to be tough, but you have a whole family here to help you pull through it."

The truck fishtailed in the snow as we powered forward and away from the prison. I didn't look back; that view was burned into my memory. My eyes focused forward where a new life waited.

"First thing on the agenda is clothes. You can't live in sweatpants and a cotton tee." Mickey turned on the radio and started to hum along with the song that was playing softly in the background.

I sat a bit taller, feeling pride at having survived the first twenty-four years of my dreadful life. In a way, I'd been reborn the minute I stepped into the frosty afternoon air. This was the first day of my new life, and no one was ever going to bully me again.

The bleak, snow-covered landscape outside the prison turned into a neighborhood of earth-colored houses, then a highway filled with colored cars, and finally, a parking lot where bold colored stores marked the beginning of endless possibilities.

Mickey pulled the truck into a slot and killed the engine. "If we can't find it here, you don't need it." She lightly elbowed me in the side. "Let's go." Mickey pushed us forward and into the department store like her hair was on fire, and the store was the only place with water. "We have hair appointments and pedicures scheduled in an hour at the spa down the street—a gift from Kerrick. He wanted to do something special for our reunion."

Mickey practically swooned when she spoke of Kerrick. She was obviously in love—she lit up like an LED at the mention of her man.

"Tell me about your men." I looked down at Holly's wedding ring and Mickey's engagement ring. "I want to hear how a real man should treat a woman, just in case I run into one. I've been told they're a dying breed."

So many women gave their men a pass when it came to deplorable behavior. And I was no exception; I spent three years justifying Tyler's horrific conduct. How many times had I convinced myself that I deserved what I got?

"The McKinley men aren't easy, but they're good men. They work hard and play harder, but they're loyal and loving." Mickey didn't need to defend her man. It was obvious he treated her well. Hell, when she smiled, she had all her teeth. The man was obviously a gem.

"Is there a McKinley for me?" I wanted a man who would treasure—not torture—me. Believe in me, not berate me. I'd never known good men. The string of losers that paraded through my childhood home terrified me. Mom was their main course, and they wanted me to be dessert. I spent most of my teenage years sleeping under my bed or tucked in the corner of my closet so they wouldn't find me. My adult years were spent much the same. "Actually, on second thought, I don't want a man. They scare the shit out of me."

"You can't judge all men by the behavior of one."

"Well,...there's Killian." Mickey shrugged her shoulders and kept walking. "He's the last remaining McKinley living on the

A Sneak Peek at Set in Stone

ranch, but..." She stopped and appeared to consider her words. "He's..."

"Rigid," Holly blurted. "He's not for you. He's too intense and a player to boot."

I looked from Holly to Mickey as they volleyed back and forth.

"Don't get us wrong," Mickey said. "He's a good guy, but he likes to be in charge, and the last thing you need is a man to dominate you."

Holly didn't miss a beat. "Outside of Killian, we have a sweet veterinarian named Roland. Then, there's Cole and the two new ranch hands, Tyson and Greer." She rushed me toward the jeans and began to pull various sizes from the racks. "Are you a six or an eight?"

My shoulders lifted. "I have no idea. Let's try an eight. I was a ten before prison, but I've shed some pounds."

"Lots can change after three years in prison—attitudes, clothes sizes, sexual preference. Look at Natalie, she traded men for women when her options were limited." Holly held up the size eight pants and nodded.

"I'm no Natalie. I could never go there. She says she closes her eyes and envisions Ryan Gosling between her legs. I suppose she has a great imagination because Debra Watson could never be mistaken for Ryan Gosling unless you're counting her facial hair." I entered the dressing room laughing. Visions of Ryan Gosling in a women's prison raced through my head. That poor man wouldn't stand a chance.

Holly followed me into the dressing room and put together outfits for me to try on. "Natalie always liked the blondes. She was dreaming of Bradley Cooper until I left." When I pulled my T-shirt over my head and let it fall to the floor, she gasped. "Oh, Megan, I'm so sorry." Her cold fingertips traced over the scars left by cigarettes and belt buckles.

"It's all behind me," I reassured her, and it was, literally. Not a blemish could be seen on the front of me. Everything I'd endured had been delivered in a cowardly fashion—behind my back, so Tyler didn't have to see my face.

A Sneak Peek at Set in Stone

Over the top of the door, lacy bras, satin bras, briefs, hipsters, and thongs in every color rained down on me. Mickey was outdoing herself in the undergarment department. I was overwhelmed by the choices and must have looked like a deer caught by a bright light. Holly shook her head and began folding the garments. "We'll take all of these. Try them all out and see which style suits you." She held up the black lace bra with fuchsia trim and smiled. "Someone is going to love this on you."

Mickey pulled the door open just as the soft blue material of the sweater draped over my hips. After a long whistle, she declared that I cleaned up nicely.

I turned to face the mirror. "I can't remember a time when my clothes fit." I rubbed my hands down my flat stomach. "The last time I wore street clothes my tummy was busting out of my pants." A tear slipped from my eye before I could wipe it away. I wrapped my arms around myself and let the tears that couldn't be contained run free.

Mickey pulled me into her arms. "That's the past, Megan. No one's asking you to forget it, but don't allow it to determine your future." She let me go, picked up the sweatpants and cotton tee I'd worn into the store and tossed them in the nearby trash can. "This is garbage. No more garbage for you. You deserve better." She pointed to the jeans and soft tunic I was wearing. "You're wearing that out. You look like million bucks wrapped in denim." She grabbed armfuls of clothes and rushed us toward the register. "We can't be late. Pampering awaits."

The cashier acted like a rabid dog when she found out that she had to scan the tags from my body, but Mickey let it drop that my last residence was the county prison. The cashier banked her irritation and hurried us through the line like we were armed and dangerous. I straightened my shoulders and stood tall in the cloud of Mickey's confidence. I'd never seen her so capable, and I said a silent prayer that someday I would have a fraction of her self-assurance.

Next stop was a drive-in for coffee. Who would have thought a girl could fall in love with a mocha latte? Men weren't necessary when you had chocolate and caffeine.

We entered the spa arm in arm. After my toes had been polished Tickle Me Pink, I was taken to the salon where a woman named Coco fondled my hair.

"What are we doin', darlin'?" She pulled me to the sink before I could answer. I was under a stream of hot water when she asked, "Do you trust me?"

"Um...yeah...I guess." What did I tell a woman who was in a position to drown me? The truth was, I didn't trust anyone except Mickey, Holly, Natalie, and Robyn. I'd been burned too many times to trust blindly, but how much trust did a hairdresser require?

She brushed and clipped until layers of soft brown hair flowed over my shoulders. If I thought a mayo rinse made my hair feel soft, whatever Coco used made my hair feel like mink—and smell like watermelon on top of that.

"You like?" Coco stood behind me with a toothy grin on her face. The girls flanked her, nodding like bobbleheads on the dashboard of a speeding car.

"Yes. I love it." I wove the soft locks between my fingers. "You made me look almost pretty." Who was this girl in front of me? I reached out to touch the mirror. She was me. I was her. We'd get through this together.

Coco shook her head. "Darlin', you were already pretty, I made your beauty shine is all." She swiped her hands back and forth and declared, "My work is done."

In a matter of hours, I had gone from a homeless waif to an attractive woman. There was no glass slipper and no pumpkin carriage, but I had two amazing fairy godmothers.

Get a free book.

Go to www.authorkellycollins.com

Other Books by Kelly Collins

The Second Chance Series

Set Free

Set Aside

Set in Stone

Set Up

Set on You

The Second Chance Series Box Set

The Boys of Fury Series

Redeeming Ryker

Saving Silas

Delivering Decker

The Boys of Fury Boxset

About the Author

International bestselling author of more than thirty novels, Kelly Collins writes with the intention of keeping love alive. Always a romantic, she blends real-life events with her vivid imagination to create characters and stories that lovers of contemporary romance, new adult, and romantic suspense will return to again and again.

For More Information
www.authorkellycollins.com
kelly@authorkellycollins.com

Printed in Great Britain
by Amazon